THE CORBIN NECKLACE

THE CORBIN NECKLACE

HENRY KITCHELL WEBSTER

WILDSIDE PRESS

Originally published in 1926.
Published by Wildside Press, LLC.
Visit us online at wildsidepress.com.

INTRODUCTION

KARL WURF

Henry Kitchell Webster (1875–1932) was a prominent American author of popular fiction during the first three decades of the twentieth century. Known for his accessible prose and interest in middle-class American life, Webster worked across several genres, including romance, social commentary, business fiction, and mystery. He often published in major periodicals of the day, and several of his works were adapted for stage and screen.

Webster's literary career began in collaboration with fellow writer Samuel Merwin; together they produced *Calumet "K"* (1901), one of the earliest and most enduring examples of the American business novel. The success of this novel, along with others such as *The Real Adventure* (1916), helped establish Webster as a reliable purveyor of moral yet entertaining fiction. His stories frequently explore personal responsibility, social ambition, and generational conflict, themes that resonated with the aspirations of early 20th-century American readers.

By the 1920s, Webster had begun exploring more overtly suspenseful plots, aligning with the rising popularity of mystery fiction in the United States. This was the era of S.S. Van Dine and Mary Roberts Rinehart, and Webster—while never part of the hardboiled school—brought his own perspective to domestic crime and family drama. In *The Corbin Necklace* (1926), a late-career work, he merges his strengths: an upper-middle-class setting, generational tension, and a central mystery rooted in family politics and the social obligations of wealth. The result is not a whodunit in the classic sense, but a psychological mystery in which character and motive take precedence over forensic clues. Webster's background in social realism gives the novel an added dimension, elevating it beyond formula.

If you want to explore Webster's other books, I recommend *Calumet "K"*, for its insight into American industrial ambition; *The Real Adventure*, which follows a woman's path to self-determination in the face of societal pressure; and *The Painted Scene* (1923), a lesser-known but well-crafted novel that blends drama and subtle suspense in a theatrical setting. Each showcases Webster's gift for character and his deep engagement with the social issues of his time.

CHAPTER I

PUNCH—AND JUDY

"How much do you suppose it's really worth?" Punch wanted to know.

"Your grandmother's necklace?" I inquired. It had been ten minutes or so since we'd mentioned it. Evidently, though, it was still on his mind. "Oh, something fabulous," I told him.

But I saw at once that the reply hadn't passed muster. It had struck him, apparently, as a typically adult remark, frivolous, or ignorant—or both. I don't like being a typical adult to Punch so I tried to do better.

"I don't know much about pearls," I said. "They're a special subject. And I haven't even seen the necklace since your mother wore it at some ball or other—oh, pre-war. Perhaps a dozen years ago. But you can put it at this, safely enough. If it were sold and the money it brought invested, even conservatively, it would produce an income one could live on."

"If you had to sell it to a fence, though," Punch observed, "you wouldn't get near so much for it. And a regular jeweler would know where it came from, if you'd stolen it, and call up the police. I suppose the way to do would be to break the string and sell the pearls one or two at a time. Even that would be pretty hard to do."

"You aren't planning to steal the necklace yourself, are you?" I inquired.

He smiled politely, by way of acknowledging the joke, but without losing his thoughtful air.

"It was horribly silly putting it in the paper, anyhow."

"Putting what in the paper?"

"About how Gran was going to give it to Judy for a wedding present. I've got it here. I tore it out of Tuesday's paper. I thought perhaps it was just as well not to have it lying around the house."

He removed it in a wad from a pocket in his knickerbockers and brought it around for me to see.

There were columns about Judith Corbin's approaching wedding in all the papers, these days. Justifiably, too, perhaps. If news is whatever people are curious about, the Corbins have been news for three generations. But the particular article which Punch had put into my hand was written in the vein

I most detest, knowing, insinuating, pandering to the most abject form of snobbery.

"Confound American newspapers!" I said.

Punch caught me up sharply. "It isn't their fault," he declared. "They're better than the newspapers in any other country."

His Americanism, I may remark, is almost rabid. As a result of his having been dragged all over Europe for most of his boyhood, the temperature of his patriotism is far above normal; say about one hundred and four. It goes rather oddly with the rest of him for in the other respects he's an incorruptible realist.

"My remark about American newspapers is stricken out," I said hastily. "I didn't mean to insult our country. But I agree with you that the reference to the necklace is unfortunate. Of course your mother...."

I was going to say, "knows best," or something like that, just to avoid any implied criticism of Victoria. But Punch broke in.

"I don't think it was mother who told them. She's been kind of funny about that necklace."

Well, there were old reasons why the necklace should be a sore point with Victoria. I didn't feel like going into them with her thirteen-year-old son.

"Where is it?" I asked. "In the bank, I suppose?"

"No, it isn't. It's down here. Grandmother's got it in that silly old safe of hers. Isn't that the worst possible place to keep anything that people might want to steal? It isn't supposed to be hard at all to open an ordinary safe. If Gran would just give it to me and let me hide it for her, somewhere, it would be a whole lot safer."

"I know," I agreed, "that in every detective story and in most plays there's a character who can sandpaper the tips of his fingers and open a safe quicker than I can break into a can of sardines. Whether experts of that sort are really so numerous, or safes so little entitled to their name, I don't know."

He didn't a bit mind my laughing at him. "Well," he said, "there's going to be big trouble, I bet, before this business is over."

Certainly there's no denying that in this instance Punch was a good prophet.

It is probably unnecessary to remark that he derives his nickname from the fact that his sister had been named Judith. He was christened John Benedict Corbin, as were his father and grandfather, both now long dead, before him. And perhaps, since I have been in a way commissioned to set down an account of the business of the next few days and the trouble it involved, I may as well begin being a little more explicit. The consensus seems to be that I know as much about it as anybody, though—or perhaps because—I have really been very little involved.

I might have been involved a good deal deeper, since I'm the Corbins' only near neighbor. The original plan had been that on the occasion of Judith's wedding—an old-style country wedding it was to be—I should keep bachelor's hall for the groom, his best man and some of the ushers. Also, as a traditional friend of the family, I'd have been over at The Oaks most of the time from the beginning of the festivities to the end. But my house, a few days earlier, had been pretty well wrecked and gutted by a bad fire, and in the course of my efforts to get things out of the burning building, I'd had the serious misfortune—that, anyhow, was the way I felt about it at the time—to break my leg.

In the light of ensuing events, I'm not altogether sorry that I had to spend those wretched days in my gardener's cottage with my leg in a cast. It had, at least, its compensations. Nobody, as far as I know, from first to last suspected me of complicity in, or even guilty knowledge of, any crime. A pair of crutches, which I was frightfully clumsy with, a twenty-pound cast on my leg and an iron-clad alibi served to protect me. And with Punch for a daily visitor, I don't think I missed much of the excitement.

It is possible that since he takes his obligations seriously, he felt he owed me something in return for the thrill he'd been afforded by my fire and my broken leg. He'd helped the surgeon put on the cast—this was before my nurse arrived—and he took a professional, almost a proprietary, interest in the damaged limb from that point on. But I'm proud to believe that Punch likes me. I'm not often, he's good enough to imply, betrayed into that levity in dealing with serious matters, to which most of my generation are incorrigibly addicted. I'm coeval more or less with his mother.

I've always known Victoria and got on with her well enough, though I never was one of her numerous adorers. Perhaps it was their numerousness that put me off. I haven't, either, in the years since her husband's death, always applauded her judgment, especially in the matter of bringing up her children. But I'd be the first to admit that she's had difficulties.

Oh well, perhaps, since I've already kept Punch waiting so long, I may as well go ahead and tell my history right end to.

The first John Corbin's father, Peter, I think his name was, came out to these parts somewhere about the time of the Black Hawk War. His ancestors had been seafaring folk—Newburyport, I think they came from—and had prospered at it. Peter had money behind him, anyhow, and he got possession of some thousands of acres of the best land in Illinois—chased the Indians off it, I suppose—and built his first house out of bricks that he made on the place.

His son, Punch's grandfather, inherited the whole thing. He may have been able enough, though I suspect the line was thinning out. Anyhow, the most important thing about him is the woman he married.

I haven't an idea who, in the social sense, she was. But certainly for the past fifty years or so she has been a tremendous person. She had two sons—she'd probably have had a dozen but for her husband's untimely death. She completely dominated the elder, Punch's father, and quarreled violently with the younger one, Alexander—she quarreled with everybody she couldn't dominate—so that he ran away, fought in the Spanish War, went out to the Philippines and stayed there.

John married Victoria Ashcroft; he died two or three months before Punch was born. Judy remembers him, of course, and adores his memory. It's one of the reasons, perhaps, why she doesn't get on better with her mother.

The proceeding years never softened up the old lady a bit. Her husband's will left the whole fortune in her hands, and she has used it remorselessly as a club to enforce submission to her ideas. In the main I think her ideas have been pretty sound—certainly her business judgment has always been above reproach—but they aren't Victoria's ideas in the least. It's hard to imagine a more difficult position than that of being old Mrs. Corbin's daughter-in-law.

The famous necklace affords an illustration. As an adornment it has long been useless to the old lady. She's been crippled with arthritis for years, living, from somewhere about dawn till nine o'clock at night, in a wheel chair. Victoria used to wear the necklace frequently. Pearls, I believe, and especially old pearls, need wear. And the thing was popularly supposed to be hers.

But between the old lady and Victoria there was never any ambiguity about it. The mother-in-law kept tabs on it most jealously; decreed when it should be worn and when it should not, and kept it most of the time in her possession. She has never liked Victoria, has often openly mistrusted her, and it was easy to believe that her decision to give the necklace to Judy was inspired by a wish to do Victoria out of it finally.

With the children Victoria more nearly had her own way. She had some money of her own, though nowhere near enough to carry out her program for them, and as long as she could keep them away from The Oaks, far enough away to sift out details, their grandmother's edicts were of little effect.

But too far Victoria dared not go. There could be no shadow of doubt that the old lady was in her right mind and able to make a will, and upon this will the disposal of the whole Corbin fortune depended. She could found a theological seminary with it if she liked.

To make it harder for Victoria—as if it weren't hard enough already—she had not, during the past three or four years, got on very well with Judy. Within the last few months we who were her friends had vaguely understood that the difficulty had got a good deal worse, and Judy was, for a while, a declared rebel. Victoria had been half frantic between the necessity of winning Judy back and keeping all echoes of the trouble from reaching Mrs. Corbin's ears. This acute phase had passed somehow, and Judy had come back, curiously sobered and, superficially at least, tractable.

Now, of course, everything was lovely. Judy was going to be married within a week to a man of whom not only her mother, but, marvelous to relate, old Mrs. Corbin as well, heartily approved.

The old lady had never seen the man himself, for she never went east, and no member of the Applebury clan had ever crossed the Alleghenies. But they were the Appleburys of East Weston, Massachusetts; cautious, solid, not too vulgarly rich. The family fortune had suffered somewhat, we understood, from their Toryism during the Revolutionary War. It was a good bet that they'd endure as long as Plymouth Rock. Anyhow, they might be supposed to be capable of managing Judy. The girl was safe now, old Mrs. Corbin thought, for life.

Victoria may have thought so too, but I take the liberty to doubt it. Safe, anyhow, probably for the next four or five years. And if there were an explosion then (I wouldn't put it by Victoria to reflect) it wouldn't so frightfully matter, since the old lady would almost certainly have been gathered to her fathers before that time.

Nunc dimittis, anyhow. For Punch would certainly never make any trouble. He could get on with anybody. Even with his grandmother.

I looked across at him now. He was lost in a brown study, probably about Monsieur Dupin or Sherlock Holmes, or some of their more recent successors.

"When are your mother and Judy coming down?" I asked.

"Oh, Judy's here," he told me. "She came yesterday afternoon. Mother was to have come with her, but she didn't. She'll come today, I expect. She'd better, because the whole gang is coming tomorrow and the house is still something awful. Decorators and curtain hangers working around all over the place. Grandmother's room is about the only one that isn't in a mess, and we're not allowed in there."

I could easily understand the need for all this renovating. The hospitality of the old house hadn't been taxed to capacity, as it was going to be for this wedding, in years.

"How is Judy?" I asked.

"All right," he said, a little doubtfully.

"Well, I assume?"

"Sure," he said.

Then he grinned. "I'd found a new way of climbing up the outside of the house—all the way to the roof. I went up yesterday, and she saw me going by her window and came out and climbed up too. Then she came all the way down. Not so bad for a girl, because there's one place where it's kind of tricky. And then we took my new rifle and shot a tin can off a fence post.

She can shoot as well as I can. I don't see what *she* wants to get married for. I don't believe she does, either."

Marriage was so evidently incomprehensible to Punch, except as a last resort after the more enjoyable resources of living had come to an end, that I didn't take this last observation so very seriously.

We were saved from discussing it by the arrival just then of Judy herself. Punch saw her before I did.

"Hello!" he exclaimed. "How did you get here?"

She came over and kissed me before she answered, and would have ignored his question altogether if he hadn't repeated it.

"Oh, in Trumble's Ford," she said. "At least I hope it was Trumble's. It was standing there in the yard where he always leaves it."

"Well," Punch said, getting up decisively, "as long as you're here, I think I'll go back."

"Brotherly love!" she commented, with a grin.

Punch explained—to me, rather than to her, "There ought to be somebody in the house."

"There were at least twenty when I left," Judy remarked. "Florists' people, upholsterers.... Heaven knows what!"

"That's why," said Punch. "Look here, I'm going to drive the Ford back. You can come along on my bike."

"I like your nerve!—Oh, it's all right. Go along."

She didn't turn back to me until she'd seen him out of the cottage and had heard the Ford go rattling away.

It didn't seem credible that she was going to be married three days from now. She looked, standing there hatless, disheveled, in her tumbled slip of a dress, not a day over fifteen. She'd been bickering with her brother like a little girl. What did she know—what could she possibly understand—about marriage?

"I had a lot of nice things all ready to say to you"—she turned back to me now with a funny little grimace of perplexity—"and Punch has put them all out of my head."

"Never mind them. And don't blame Punch. He's worrying about the famous necklace."

"Oh, damn the necklace!" she cried.

She might well enough have used an exclamation like that offhand, humorously, or by way of experiment to see if I'd be shocked. But she didn't use it in any of these ways. The thing had struck a nerve somehow.

"That's a reasonable enough wish," I said, "on general principles. But why particularly?"

"Did you see that silly story in the paper?" she asked. "About how Gran was going to give it to me for a wedding present? It gave mother a jolt, all right, when she read it yesterday at breakfast."

"She hadn't wanted it published, then?"

Judy stared. "Wanted it published? It was the first she'd heard of it. And—well, she didn't seem quite to know whether to believe me or not when I said I hadn't heard about it either. I told her it must be just a newspaper guess. She's always thought grandmother ought to give it to her. And of course she ought. I told mother I didn't want it myself. If it was mine, the first thing I'd do with it would be to sell it. Heavens! Think of having a thing around your neck or on your dressing-table that was worth—how much? Fifty thousand dollars?"

"More like twice that, I suppose," I told her.

She shivered.

"Well, I tried to talk mother out of it, but I couldn't. She wouldn't believe it was just a mare's nest, whether it was news to me or not. And she isn't really sure it was."

"What does your grandmother say about it?"

"Oh, I haven't seen her since I came down. Miss Digby won't let me in. I suppose this happens to be one of the times when she isn't—presentable."

I was rather aghast at that, and I dare say I showed it. Judy gave me an intent look, and went on.

"You knew that, didn't you? That she—takes something? Oh, I don't know what. Morphine, I suppose. Heaven knows I don't blame her! I'd do it if I were in her fix. Hope she'll be all right for the wedding. Probably will be. I suppose old Digs is just tuning her up."

She didn't look like a child as she said that.

Suddenly she came over and sat down on the edge of my couch, took one of my hands and patted it.

"Do you want to hear all about the plans for the wedding, who the bridesmaids are, and what they're going to wear—the sort of man I'm going to marry...."

"Tell me that," I broke in. "What's Bruce Applebury like?"

She considered silently before she answered. But there was nothing about her unsmiling young face to suggest the sort of reverie a young girl in love might be expected to fall into over such a question.

"I won't try it," she said at last. "It's too important a subject. You'll see him anyhow in a day or two. I'll bring him over and give you a look."

She wasn't quite willing to let it go at that, however.

"He's all right—abso*lute*ly."

The mispronunciation was humorously meant, or, rather, was meant to sound as if it were. But people with finely expressive voices like Judy's inevitably give themselves away. I stirred with an involuntary protest. It was an outrage, marrying her off like that—a girl of twenty—to a man she was not in love with.

She plunged into a detailed recital of the festivities, and never paused until she got up to go.

"So you see all the fun you're going to miss for having broken your poor old leg? Oh, but your nose would have been out of joint anyway. You were to have given me away, you know. But it seems it's going to be Uncle Alec."

"Not Alexander Corbin!" I exclaimed. "Where in the world has he turned up from?"

"From the Philippines, where he's been all the time. Mother got a telegram Saturday from San Francisco. That was something of a jolt too, I expect. You'll come over for the wedding itself, though, won't you, on Saturday afternoon—in a horse litter or a palanquin, or something?"

I told her I would.

In the doorway she paused for a comprehensive glance about the room. "It's a nice little room, isn't it," she said. "And a nice little house. I've never been in here before."

She paused a moment, then went on. "The horridest thing in the world, I'm getting to think, is whitewash, and it's going to be thick over at The Oaks this week. I'm going to be coated with it. Come out looking like a nice little plaster angel. Do you know what I'd like to do? I'd like to poison your nurse, or something, and come down here and take care of you—for the rest of this week."

"And not get married at all?" I asked.

"They used to do that by proxy sometimes, didn't they? I should think that would be a good way to do it. Good-by. I suppose Punch left his bicycle around here somewhere."

I tried, after she'd gone, to make myself believe that there was nothing to this but the modern young girl's dread of seeming to be the conventional blushing bride, but I couldn't manage it. Punch's prediction that there was going to be big trouble before this business was over stuck in my mind like a burr.

CHAPTER II

SHOAL WATER

Punch's sense of duty condemned him to a rather dull day. He ate a solitary lunch, for his mother hadn't returned from town, and Judy was apparently making a day of it with his bicycle. He spent several uneventful hours wandering over the house, watching workmen and servants going about their duty, but without detecting anything that looked suspicious. Of course he couldn't be everywhere at once.

The Oaks is an enormous house; old, as such matters are reckoned out in this part of the world. It was built about fifty years ago, of dark red brick with Gothic trimmings in wood, three stories high, and a nervous-looking, high peaked roof on top of that.

Structurally it hasn't been altered very much, save for additional bathrooms, the installation of electric lights and an elaborate system of burglar alarms. The place is a regular fort. One incongruous innovation, namely an elevator, was necessitated by old Mrs. Corbin's illness. She might, of course, have moved down to rooms on the ground floor, but she wasn't willing to do that. She said she'd lived in those rooms ever since she came to the house as a bride and she was going to die in them. She'd have found it unendurable, too, no doubt, to give up the possibility of visiting any room in her house; seeing to it that the house-maids did their duty.

It abounded, of course, in odd, unused and half-forgotten nooks and crannies. On a rainy day Punch found endless enjoyment in exploring these, and he probably knew more about the house, little of his life as he had spent in it, than anybody else, his grandmother included.

The old lady appeared for the first time that day about four o'clock. She impressed Punch as unusually bright, and in the main, good-humored, although her dismissal of poor Miss Digby at sight of him was brusk, and her comments on his mother's continued absence decidedly caustic. She put him in charge of her wheel chair, and elected to make a tour of the house to see how things were going. There were still workmen on every floor, but it began to look as if they were going to finish in time.

From the wheel chair she allotted the rooms for her expected guests, from memory. Although she forgot some of them, and her plans had to be heavily revised, it struck the boy as a remarkable evidence, not only of her disposition to run things, but of her ability to do so. His mother wouldn't have been capable of it, he felt pretty sure. But of course she'd never have tried to do it without a list.

The outline of the scheme was simple enough. The unmarried men, groom, best man, ushers and odd relations, such as Punch's mysterious Uncle Alec, were to have the top floor. Punch's own quarters were up there. The middle of this story was a billiard room. It was surrounded by a regular rabbit warren of bedrooms and the only daylight it got came from a big window on the landing of the stairs.

Married couples, maiden aunts, bridesmaids and so on had their rooms on floors below.

Punch found all these decisions and indecisions rather stupid—his thoughts remained on the necklace—and when the tour of inspection was finally finished and his grandmother returned to her own sitting-room, he tactfully brought up the subject by asking her how old she supposed the safe was and whether his grandfather had bought it. It was a rather big old-fashioned affair of cast iron, lacquered, and with a picture of a startled stag painted on the door—one of the first works of art that Punch had ever admired.

"Yes, your grandfather bought it," the old lady admitted. "And it's a good safe, too. They don't make things as well as that now-a-days."

"Perhaps not," Punch agreed. "But I think they make them harder to break into. I read in a magazine a while ago that any safe more than ten years old might just as well be left unlocked, as far as burglars were concerned."

"Well, I don't leave this one unlocked," his grandmother said grimly, "burglars or no. What are you getting at, you young rascal? Still thinking about that necklace?"

Punch admitted that he was.

"Like a look at it?" she asked.

Would he!

He darted over to the safe. "Let me unlock it, Gran," he pleaded. "Tell me the combination. See if I can do it."

"You let it alone," she ordered. "I'll do it myself."

She began wheeling her chair across the room, but the next moment Punch had turned the handle and pulled the great door open.

"Why, Gran," he cried, horrified, "it wasn't locked!"

The pearls, like all the other contents of the irregularly shelved, cubbyholed place, were safe all right, and as soon as this had been discovered to be a fact, the old lady tried hard to convince her grandson that she had known that it was unlocked all the time. But he knew that for a minute she had been absolutely incapacitated by terror, and the look in her withered old face was one that he didn't like to remember. She had simply forgotten to lock the safe the last time she'd gone to it. She was too badly shaken to do anything for herself. Even after he'd found the long morocco covered box in the place she'd indicated, she was too weak to press the spring that released the lid.

Punch found the pearls rather disappointing. They were beautiful, of course. Big and round and handsome, and rather nice to touch. But as anything to commit a crime for, or to pay a fortune for, he couldn't see it. He was too polite to express these opinions to his grandmother, who he perceived was deeply moved by the sight of the thing.

She told him a long history of the necklace, the occasion of his grandfather's buying it, and the admiration it had excited on various memorable occasions.

"Are you really going to give it to Judy?" he asked.

"What's that about Judy?" she demanded.

She wasn't deaf a bit, he was sure, but she often asked to have things repeated. His theory of this was that it gave her more time to decide what she wanted to say.

"It was in the paper yesterday," he explained, "that you were going to give the necklace to Judy for a wedding present."

He extricated from his pocket the same damp wad of paper he had offered for my inspection that morning. She didn't pretend to read it, though. Her vision wasn't nearly so good as her hearing, and without her spectacles, which she hated to wear, she couldn't read at all.

"So they had it in the paper, did they?" she remarked. "Well, it's an amazing thing how much these newspaper reporters know. What has Judy got to say about it?"

"She hasn't said anything to me," Punch told her.

"How about your mother? I dare say she had some ideas on the subject."

"I haven't seen mother," Punch pointed out to her, "since she went to town with Judy last week. But what I thought was that as long as it did come out in the paper, it would be better to hide these where no one would think of looking for them, instead of leaving them in the safe, which is the first place where any one would look. Especially while there are so many people we don't know around the house. I *know* I could hide them, Gran, where they'd be safe."

He had an idea that she was considering the proposal favorably. At any rate she didn't at once decline it. But in the middle of the silence there came a light tap on the door.

Punch admits that he jumped a little himself, for they hadn't heard any footsteps. His grandmother started violently, then called, "Who's there?"

"It's Victoria," Punch heard his mother say. "May I come in?"

He thought his grandmother made a move to put the pearls back in the safe, but she changed her mind, and answered rather sharply, "Yes, of course. Come in."

He thought the sight of the pearls surprised his mother.

"Letting Punch have a gloat over them, are you?" she said. "I've had a frightful ride out from town. That's a beastly train. I suppose," she went on, reverting to the necklace, "that you've heard what was in the paper. They say you're going to give them to Judy for a wedding present."

"So Punch has just been telling me," his grandmother remarked dryly.

She didn't add anything to that, and Punch looked over at his mother. He got the queer impression that she was holding her breath. She seemed awfully tired and worried, anyway.

"Well," she said at last, "I suppose that sort of irresponsibility is what we have to expect from the papers. Unless," she went on jerkily, after another pause, "this happens to be the truth."

"I can make it the truth if I like," the old woman said.

"Yes, of course," his mother remarked. "No one questions that."

Punch was getting uncomfortable. It's horribly embarrassing to children to be present when their elders quarrel, and of course he was sensitive enough to feel electricity in the air. He brought the lightning down upon himself.

"Well, they can't be given to Judy if they're stolen by a burglar first," he pointed out. "Won't you let me have them, Gran, to hide for you?"

She turned upon him furiously. "No, I will not! And I won't be nagged to death about them either, by you or by any one else."

She whipped around on her daughter-in-law. "Why shouldn't I give them to Judy?" she demanded. "She's my own granddaughter, isn't she?"

"Judy says she doesn't want them ..." his mother began.

But his grandmother pounced upon her again.

"You've been trying to talk her out of it, have you? So that you could get them for yourself? Well, that settles it. She shall have them whether she wants them or not. And once she's married you'll find her husband will have something to say about what she does with them. I won't hear another word about them. Ring for Miss Digby, Punch."

She wheeled her chair forward, restored the pearls to the safe, tugged shut, with a good deal of trouble, the big iron door herself, waving off their proffered assistance, and spun the combination knob.

"Don't try to tell me I don't keep this locked," she said.

The thing that seemed to be puzzling Punch, when he reported the scene to me, was his grandmother's sudden change of mind about confiding the pearls to him.

"I think she really meant to let me hide them," he said. "Anyhow she didn't get mad when I suggested it the first time. But the second time she pretty near blew me out of the room."

I didn't offer the boy the upshot of my own speculations, which was that a sudden suspicion had sprung up in the old woman's mind that her grandson was in league with his mother, and that the original suggestion, that he be given the pearls to hide, had come from her.

Punch didn't see anything more of his mother that day, until he came down into the drawing-room dressed for dinner, where he found her talking to Judy. They went right on talking, somewhat enigmatically, after they'd seen him come in, so he had felt entitled to listen and make what he could of it.

They both looked as if the conversation had been rather exciting. But Judy was speaking now more affectionately than was her wont. It was as if they'd made up a quarrel about something.

"But of *course* I will, mother! I understand, and I'll do it exactly. You leave it to me. I won't give anybody a chance at it, old Eagle-Eye or any one else. And please don't bother about it, mother. It isn't as if I cared."

"You're a queer child," her mother said. "Is it really true that you don't care?"

"Not the smallest conceivable—damn!" said Judy. She smiled a very small smile, and added "I don't know about Bruce, though. You may have to square me with him."

"You'll have no trouble squaring yourself with him," her mother told her.

There must have been, Punch thought, some significance in the words that Judy didn't like, for she turned sharply away, and he saw that her face had flushed.

But Uncle Alec came into the room just then and that talk was over. He'd arrived only about an hour before.

Punch was inclined to approve of his long lost uncle. He was quite jolly, and kept them entertained through what would otherwise have been a pretty painful dinner, with Gran up at the head of the table still in the frame of mind she'd been in after her quarrel with her daughter-in-law. He told them about his tobacco plantation, and his plans for growing rubber, and spun a few delightfully bloodcurdling tales about Moros and Igorots.

Then, just as everything was going so well, he went off the deep end by saying something about Judy's necklace. He'd been reading yesterday's paper in the train.

Punch didn't know how the quarrel flared up again. Everybody went on trying to be polite for a while, but it wasn't long before the fat was in the fire. He fastened his eyes upon his plate and tried not to listen to the blistering things his grandmother was saying. Uncle Alec was horrified, of course.

He did his best to pacify his mother, but without avail. And finally Punch's mother got up and left the room. He wasn't surprised. He only wondered that she'd stood it as long as she did.

He didn't see her again that evening, and when he came down to breakfast next day Belden, the old butler, told him she'd gone to town on the early train and was coming back with the guests on the special car that afternoon.

She hated the journey to town, he knew, and he thought it rather funny that she should undertake it again on a hot morning like this, the very day that most of their guests, including the Applebury clan, were coming down.

I silently agreed with him—more heartily than I was willing to admit. There were several things that looked rather queer to me. I couldn't resist asking a question or two.

"Have you seen Judy this morning?"

He shook his head. "I haven't seen anybody but Uncle Alec. He was down to breakfast and we walked around the place for a while, afterward. He asked me about a million questions. I like him, though."

I wanted to know what he looked like.

"Oh, kind of peaceful and jolly. But he sees things quickly enough. I told him about where Gran keeps the necklace. I sort of left him in charge so that I could come over here."

"You don't think," I hazarded, "that he was the person Judy meant by 'old Eagle-Eye'?"

He looked rather thoughtful over that but said he didn't. "Somehow he isn't like that. Anyhow, I thought she was talking about the man she's going to marry—Bruce Applebury."

This didn't strike me as likely. The adjective old, for instance. Applebury was under thirty. But then Judy, like Punch himself, wouldn't hesitate to apply it to anyone over twenty-five.

I grew more apprehensive and indignant as I turned the matter over in my mind after Punch had gone back "on the job," as he said. Victoria was in shoal water of some sort. There couldn't be any doubt of that. Academically speaking, I was sorry for her. But I had no sympathy with what seemed like an attempt to drag Judy into the breakers with her.

Oh yes, I'm sentimental about Judy. I may as well admit that at once.

CHAPTER III

FRUSTRATION OF PUNCH

None of the Corbins went down to the village, which is the better part of two miles from The Oaks, to meet the train. Both Gran and Uncle Alec seemed to think it rather queer that Judy didn't plan to go, but she explained her position with perfect lucidity.

"We've hardly been able to scrape up cars enough to bring them all out in one trip. And mother will be there, of course, to do the arranging."

"Won't your young man feel a bit defrauded at not finding you there?" Uncle Alec asked her.

"It's hard to know about that," Judy answered him thoughtfully. "That's another reason. You see, I don't know whether he'd expect me to kiss him on the station platform or not. I think it's safer, on the whole, to wait and do it here."

The train happened to be late, and they waited quite a while—Gran, Uncle Alec, Judy and Punch in the corner of one of the deep verandas that commanded the drive. At last the first car appeared.

"There's Bruce," Judy said. "He's the one in the front seat."

She turned to her brother with a funny sort of smile, and added, "So it looks as if it were really going to happen, Punch."

He found, to his consternation, that he had a lump in his throat and he turned away from her quickly to watch the approaching car. She'd upset him horribly, somehow, looking at him like that. It seemed contrary to the laws of nature that that rather good-looking, plump-faced, slightly pompous grown-up could seriously be planning to carry Judy away to live with him. Judy!

The boy's impulse was to grab her by the arm, drag her around the corner of the house, and bolt with her. Hide somewhere until the excitement had blown over. There were plenty of girls whom no one would miss who might be allowed to marry Mr. Applebury if they liked.

But Judy wouldn't go with him, he realized, even if he did grab her arm. She'd said good-by to him, somehow, in that one look.

He watched her as she moved off, composedly enough, to meet the car under the porte-cochère. He saw Bruce spring spryly out; he heard Judy's short little laugh just before she kissed him. Then she turned quickly and began greeting the others. Now they were all coming up into the veranda together, toward the group of three that remained in the corner.

A saving idea occurred to Punch. His grandmother's room up-stairs had been left unguarded now for a long while. Most of the servants were having lunch; everybody else had been occupied expecting the arriving guests. Sentry duty was his job now. He slipped around the corner of the veranda, entered the house and stole swiftly up the stairs.

The upper hall was deserted. He tried the door to his grandmother's room. It wasn't locked, and he went in, crossed over to the safe and tried the door to that. It was locked all right, so he withdrew to the hall again. Down at the end of it stood a big high-sided davenport. It afforded an excellent post of observation, since by crouching down in the lee of one of the great arms one could make one's self highly unnoticeable, almost invisible.

Through the open windows he could hear cars arriving, one after another, and a steadily rising surge of voices. Sometimes he could isolate Judy's. Once or twice he heard her laugh. Still the cars kept arriving. Lord, there were a lot of people! And there would be still more tomorrow.

He stayed there for what seemed quite a long while, but it couldn't have been, really, because, of course, as soon as the baggage had come up from the station, the servants would begin carrying up suit-cases and things to the different rooms.

Presently he heard a step on the stair, coming up in a hurry but quietly. Instantly he was at gaze, breathless to see who would appear around the turn of the landing. It was Judy.

He'd have spoken to her if astonishment had not silenced him. Her face was so white that the color she had put on it stood out unnaturally, and her eyes were wild, like those of a frightened animal.

She looked right at him as she passed, and he thought at first she hadn't seen him at all. But when she went into her room she left the door open behind her and called his name, not loud, but urgently.

"Come in," she said, as he halted on the threshold, "and shut the door after you."

She had flung herself down on the bed. He stood awkwardly beside her, not knowing what he ought to do. She wasn't crying. He thought she must be suddenly ill.

"Hadn't I better call mother?" he asked.

"No," she said. "Don't call anybody. Don't do anything. Just stay here a few minutes until I have had time to think. Sit down and give me something to hold on to. It's rocking like a boat."

She clutched the hand he gave her with a strength that hurt, and the coldness of hers frightened him. But he obeyed her literally and didn't try to talk, let alone ask questions.

Presently her grip relaxed and her eyes steadied themselves. Evidently the rocking wasn't quite so bad. She had a queer look in her face, though there was nothing you could call it but a smile. And then suddenly her eyes filled up with tears and she began to cry. She buried her face in a pillow in order to make no noise, and sobbed and shook. But this somehow didn't distress him as much as the smile had done.

The crying didn't last very long, and when it was finished and she looked up at him again and said shakily, "I'm all right now," he perceived that this was true.

"I don't know what I'm going to do," she said. "I've got to think and I can't, yet. Punch, are you for me? Are you on my side whatever happens—whatever I do?"

"Sure I am!" he told her.

"Sure you are!" she said, and sitting up suddenly, she kissed him in the sort of brief, businesslike way that was her fashion.

Then she dropped back again on the pillow.

"Why, this is what happened," she went on, after a thoughtful silence. "You're to go down now and tell them all about it. I slipped on a rug, down there in the hall, and turned my ankle, quite hard. And I'm up here now in my bathroom putting it in hot water so it won't be swollen—for the wedding, you know. And I shan't be able to play tennis this afternoon, or swim either, I suppose. But otherwise I'm quite all right. You don't mind being a liar, do you, Punch, in a good cause?"

He told her he didn't.

"Where did you disappear to when the crowd came?" she asked him suddenly. "You were there just the minute before."

"Oh, I was sort of keeping an eye on things," he told her. "Grandmother's room, you know. On account of the necklace."

She gave a rather sudden laugh at that, and told him he had that necklace on the brain.

"Forget it!" she commanded him. "Go down and meet the Appleburys. But don't forget about my ankle."

Punch got down-stairs in time to find the crowd on the veranda in the act of dispersal to their rooms. He gave Judy's message to his mother, and it had, of course, the effect of checking, for a few minutes, the movement indoors. People crowded around, plying him for details, and passing the news along.

He was a little uneasy at first from the impression that he had seen a flicker of incredulity in his mother's eye, but elsewhere belief seemed instantaneous. He avoided elaborating the story, though. He knew only what Judy had told him. He added one small lie of his own. He said he hadn't seen the ankle himself. She'd been talking to him through the bathroom door.

It was hard luck, they all felt, but there was nothing to be done about it. They might as well go in and dress for tennis or riding, or just lounging about. Punch was requisitioned as usher to show people where their rooms were.

When he had personally conducted a good many of them and the rush was over, he came down-stairs from the third floor to find a man he hadn't previously seen, standing about indecisively in the second-floor hall.

"I seem to have got lost," he said to the boy. "I'm William Grant, a cousin of Bruce Applebury. You're Punch, aren't you?"

Punch said he was, and took the hand the man held out to him.

"Why, you're up in what we call The Club," he said. "That's on the next floor. I'll show you."

"I don't believe that's necessary," the man protested. "I think I can find it if you'll tell me."

"Oh, no," Punch insisted. "I'll show you. Come along."

He was deeply perplexed as he turned to mount the stairs. There was nothing queer of course about his having failed to see the man in the crowd on the veranda. There was no reason to doubt his being a wedding guest. He looked like a person who would be one. Punch had liked his looks instantly. He looked sort of lazy, and yet alert too, and as if he was the kind of person that could understand things.

But what he hadn't in the least looked like, in the moment when Punch first glimpsed him in the hall, was a man who had lost his way and was looking for the door of his own room. It had looked more like waiting than looking. A rather exciting sort of waiting, too.

Had he been a little reluctant to accept Punch's guidance? Hadn't he hung back a little, for one last glance around that hall that Gran's door opened into?

This must have been pure imagination on Punch's part. There was no mystery about the man's identity at all events. He was Bruce Applebury's cousin, all right.

The Club was what they called an irregular suite of three or four bedrooms and a bath, opening through a tiny vestibule of its own into the billiard room. As Punch opened the door and conducted the man in, they saw the prospective bridegroom, already stripped to his underclothes, and getting out of them for his bath.

Punch had to revise one of his estimates immediately. There was nothing fat or soft about Judy's fiancé. What gave him that stout look was clear muscle. He was a much more impressive and formidable-looking figure like this than when he was covered up with clothes.

"Where in the world have you been?" he said to Punch's charge.

"Got lost," the other said cheerfully. "Punch, here, rescued me."

"Well, look alive," Bruce commanded, "if you're going to play tennis."

"I'm not," his cousin told him. "Changed my mind."

"How's Judy?" Bruce asked Punch. "Has she come out yet?"

Punch said he didn't think so. He hadn't seen her, anyhow.

"It's a shame you won't be able to see her play, Bill. Her form's simply immense, and she gets around the court like a little wildcat."

Punch knew he didn't like Bruce Applebury when he heard him say this. He was talking already as if he owned her. And what was rather strange, he got the impression that Bill Grant didn't like it very well either.

He was feeling rather silly as he came down-stairs from The Club over having doubted Bill Grant's authenticity as a cousin of the bridegroom and having almost suspected him of being a burglar. He had half a mind to try to do as Judy had commanded and forget the necklace. But to his orderly young mind this would have been impossible. He simply couldn't leave loose ends.

So he crossed to his grandmother's door and knocked lightly. He didn't suppose she was there, for she seldom came down-stairs but once before dinner. He just wanted to make sure, once more, that everything was all right. He was on the point of letting himself in, since no voice answered his knock, when he heard footsteps. The door was opened, and he was confronted by Miss Digby. She had a sort of harassed, interrupted air as she opened the door, and it changed to something like exasperation when she saw who the visitor was.

"What do you want?" she demanded. She didn't offer to let him in.

"Nothing," he told her truthfully. "I just wanted to make sure that everything was all right."

"Oh, Punch," she cried, "go away! Stop bothering about that necklace. Your grandmother's just come up to lie down. She's going to rest until dinner time. The strain of meeting so many people was a little too much for her. So don't be a nuisance if you can help it."

"All right," he said, "I won't;" and she closed the door.

He hung about the upper hall for a little while hoping, since Judy's door was half open, that she would come out, but she didn't, so he went forlornly out to the court.

His spirits came up, little by little, out here in the sunshine. There was a lot of good fast tennis. Applebury played insatiably; a hard, wary, efficient sort of game. It was evident he loved it. Punch kept an eye open for Bill Grant, who he hoped would appear among the onlookers, but in this he was disappointed.

He saw him later, though, at the pool, when the tennis was over. Everybody went in then, including Punch himself. Judy, with a cane, and a good big bandage showing through her stocking, came down to watch the sport. She gave so good an imitation of a girl with a damaged ankle that Punch found himself wondering whether perhaps it hadn't been true that she'd slipped on the rug. And certainly there seemed to be nothing now the matter with her spirits. He was heavily at a discount with himself as a detective when he went into the house to dress for dinner.

This didn't take him long—all his movements are singularly neat and swift—and he was the first person to come down from the top floor.

His grandmother's door was open now and when he paused there a moment she called to him to come in. She was dressed for dinner and all ready for her ride down in the elevator. She struck him, just as she had on her first appearance the day before, as being rather unusually bright-looking somehow. And again almost unnaturally amiable.

"How about it, Punch?" she asked. "Shall we give your sister something to make up to her for her bad ankle? Nobody will look at her ankles if she has the pearls around her neck. Why shouldn't she wear them tonight? Give that bridegroom of hers a treat. Let him see what he's going to get."

Punch was moved to protest. "I sort of don't think she'd want to wear them tonight," he said. "It's nearly two whole days before the wedding."

"Go and call her," his grandmother commanded, starting to wheel herself over to the safe. "No, don't stop to help me. I don't need it. Go tell your sister as soon as she's dressed to come to me."

Punch went on the errand a little reluctantly, and gave the message to Judy through the door.

He meant to dart back to his grandmother's room in time to see her open the safe. He was curious as to whether this time it was locked or not. But Judy detained him.

"I'll go now," she said. "I'm dressed all but my dress, and I don't want to put that on till it's time to go down to dinner. Come in here a minute."

She was putting on, as he entered the room, some sort of kimono-like garment of orange-colored silk. But she arrested the action to laugh at the sight of him.

"You look so nice and innocent, with your hair brushed," she explained, and having her arms in her sleeves by this time, she came over and hugged him. "Oh, Punch, you're a dear," she cried. "You made an instantaneous hit this afternoon. Do you know that?"

It wasn't the caress that made him uncomfortable, nor yet the compliment. It was the sort of wildness there was about her look.

"I don't know what's going to happen," she went on, still holding him by the shoulders and looking at him very intently. "I don't know that it matters—much—what does. Only—you haven't forgotten what you said this afternoon? You're on my side, you know."

He told her that he was and that he hadn't forgotten.

"All right," she said. "Come along to grandmother. Do you know what she wants?"

He was afraid, somehow, that if he told her she'd refuse, so instead of answering her question he reminded her that she was starting off without her cane. She laughed and darted across the room to get it. Then, with her arm through his, she limped decorously down the hall to her grandmother's room.

The old lady had opened the safe door, and had the brown morocco case in her lap.

"That isn't your dinner dress, is it?" she complained at sight of her granddaughter. "I sent word you were to come when you were dressed. I wanted to see how you'd look in the pearls. However, now you're here, you may as well put them on."

Punch had been watching his sister, for the sight of the morocco case in his grandmother's lap had convinced him that everything was all right. He saw her eyes widen a little.

At the same moment his grandmother uttered a wheezy sort of shriek. He turned and looked. The box she held in her hand was empty.

"Shut the door!" Judy commanded, and his prompt obedience came none too soon, for with the old woman's next breath she cried out, full voice, "They're gone. She's taken them. Your mother's taken them."

"Are they *really* gone?" Judy asked.

Then to Punch's amazement she began to laugh.

CHAPTER IV

SOMETHING BEHIND

I had three visitors that evening. Punch was the first. He ditched the dinner at The Oaks and rode over on his bicycle in time to dine with me—to go through the motions of dining with me, rather, for he ate hardly anything.

He was, of course, terribly cast down by the loss of the necklace which he had tried so conscientiously to guard. He felt, too, that if the others had treated the case as seriously as he had done, it needn't have happened. They hadn't treated it seriously, none of them, with the exception of Uncle Alec. They'd laughed at him for having the necklace on the brain. They'd implored him to forget it and not be a pest.

He didn't, though, entirely acquit himself of negligence. That half-hour or more while they had waited in the veranda for the arrival of the guests, he himself with the others, might have given the thief, assuming that he'd secreted himself in the house at some time previously, his opportunity. And this was just the time, Punch said, when he should have been on the job.

"Oh, come!" I protested. "There were plenty of other chances for the thing to be taken. You couldn't have stayed on guard all the time."

He insisted with a vehemence which didn't strike me as quite like him that this was when the necklace had disappeared.

"The necklace is known to have been seen," I argued, "by nobody since your grandmother showed it to you yesterday afternoon. She put it back in the safe and locked it up. It seems to me our difficulty is that there have been so many chances to take it."

"For who to take it?" he asked me.

"Why, for almost anybody who was in the house," I said.

A queer look went over his face, as if that off-hand remark of mine had frightened him.

"Not for any one who *would* take it," he said. "Of course there were chances for people who wouldn't."

At that I got an idea. I asked him suddenly, "How do you know that the necklace has really been taken? Your grandmother sprang the loss of it on you and Judy in a rather dramatic way. Isn't it possible that she adopted your idea that the jewels ought to be hidden somewhere rather than kept in the safe? She'd been rather annoyed at your insistence that they oughtn't to be in the safe, although she'd become convinced, more or less, that you were right about it. She'd been still more annoyed at Judy for saying she didn't want the necklace.

"Well, then, she sends you to get Judy, opens the safe, tucks the pearls away somewhere—in her own dress perhaps—and then springs the empty box on the pair of you. Isn't that possible? She has guarded against their being stolen, and she's scored off you and Judy at the same time."

"She wasn't paying any attention to Judy and me. She didn't even notice that Judy laughed. She was screaming that mother had taken them. Practically out of her head. Miss Digby had to give her a hypodermic to quiet her."

That shattered my theory. It had been no joke, even of the grimmest, for the old woman. But my mind had already fastened on something else.

"Judy laughed, you say, when she saw that the necklace was gone?"

He hadn't told me that before.

"Yes," he said.

I remarked that it was natural enough that she should be a bit hysterical for the moment after a loss of that kind.

"That wasn't the *way* she laughed," he told me. "She laughed as if it was something that didn't matter very much, but was rather funny. As if she was really thinking about something else. But I don't know why she laughed nor what the other thing was she was thinking about."

His voice had faltered, but he had forced it to the end of the sentence, and I perceived what I might have guessed earlier. The thing the boy was agonizing over lay deeper than the disappearance of the necklace, although behind it perhaps, and connected with it.

"Well," I said cheerfully, "we know Judy didn't steal the necklace anyway, nor your mother, either. Go back to the time the people came and tell me everything that's happened."

It steadied him to have a piece of perfectly straight reporting like that to do; something that called the faculties of his active, orderly mind into play, and he went ahead and gave me the narrative of the afternoon, substantially as I have put it down in the preceding chapter. I didn't interrupt him with questions. But when he had finished I asked a few.

"Miss Digby wouldn't have stayed in the room while your grandmother was lying down, would she?"

"Not in her bedroom," he said. "But it's her sitting-room next door where the safe is. I thought she was going to stay in the sitting-room, but I'm not sure she did."

"If she went away," I pointed out, "there'd have been a chance for someone to open the safe if it weren't locked, or to unlock it if he knew the combination, and get the necklace while your grandmother was asleep. For that matter, isn't it likely that Miss Digby knows the combination to the safe herself? She must have seen your grandmother open it a hundred times."

"Yes," he said, "I suppose she does." Then he laughed. "Old Digs didn't take the necklace though," he said.

I agreed with him about that. It wasn't possible seriously to suspect Miss Digby.

"I'm not talking about the probability that any one stole it," I explained. "I'm trying to include all the people who had a chance to take the necklace at that time."

"Well," he said, "if Digs went out, everybody who was in the house had a chance."

"Including," I remarked, "your assumed thief who had concealed himself somewhere on the premises."

"It wouldn't have been so good a chance for him as the other time," he insisted, "because Judy was right there in her room across the hall, and her door was open when Miss Digby sent me away. Besides, there were a lot of people down-stairs all the rest of the afternoon. He'd have had trouble getting away without meeting anybody."

"What are they doing about it?" I asked. "How many people know the necklace is gone?"

"Only mother and Uncle Alec, besides Gran and Judy and me. Oh, and Digs, of course. I went and got mother and she sent me for Uncle Alec. They jawed about it, there in grandmother's room, until it was time to go down to dinner."

"Didn't your grandmother herself have anything to say about it?"

"Oh, she was in bed in the next room. The hypodermic put her out, I guess. It was mostly mother and Uncle Alec. He's awfully excited about it. Wants to send for detectives. But mother won't have it."

"How about Judy?" I asked. "You'd think her vote would count, as long as it was to have been her necklace."

"Judy didn't vote. She didn't seem to care what they did. It seemed as if she was still thinking about something else. I don't think she wanted the police, though."

"What do *you* want?" I asked.

The intensity of his answer startled me.

"I don't care much about the necklace now," he said, "but I want the thief found. *I'm* not afraid who it'll turn out to be."

"You mean," I asked, "that you think your mother and Judy *are* afraid?"

He looked at me steadily but did not answer.

Possibly to his relief, and certainly to my own, we heard a car door slam just then, and Punch darted to the window to see who it was.

"Here's mother now," he said, and went to open the door for her.

I couldn't see her face when she perceived her small son, but of course I heard what she said to him.

"Oh, you're here, are you? We were wondering what had become of you."

Her tone was composed, almost good-natured, but rather cold. My guess is she was glad she was saved the trouble of telling me what had happened, but at the same time a little put out by this indication that I was deep in Punch's confidence. He was always rather reticent with her.

After she'd come into my sitting-room and greeted me, she turned back to him. "Run along home now," she said curtly, "and tell Judy I'll be back in fifteen minutes."

He obeyed her with alacrity; he barely nodded a farewell to me as he said, "All right, mother," and disappeared. If he felt any curiosity as to our interview, he didn't show it. I think he was glad just then not to talk to her.

She did the polite thing by my broken leg, helped herself, at my invitation, to one of my cigarettes, and settled down, with a deep-drawn, very audible sigh, in the big chair which Punch had just vacated.

"I suppose you know," she said, "the ghastly thing that's just happened over at The Oaks?"

"I know as much about it as Punch knows," I said somewhat tentatively.

As a matter of fact, Victoria herself had astonished me. For in spite of her sigh and her use of the word ghastly to describe the theft, her manner was almost complacent.

It seemed incredible that this should be so, but there was no getting away from it. The mental picture I'd formed of her during the past couple of days, derived mostly from the reports I'd been getting from Punch, had been of a woman driven half frantic by worry, involved in some sort of dangerous web.

The web appeared, certainly, to be woven about the necklace. She had, according to Judy, sustained a shock when she read in the paper that it was to be given to her daughter as a wedding present. She'd quarreled furiously with old Mrs. Corbin about it. It had caused—apparently, at least, it was the thing that had caused—sudden alterations in her plans. I had taken for granted, though on insufficient evidence perhaps, that it was the theme of that mysteriously emotional conversation with Judy, which Punch had heard the end of, on the night of Alexander Corbin's arrival.

Yet now, within a couple of hours of the discovered theft of the precious dangerous thing, she sat there looking at me as calm and contented as a cat who had just licked the meringue off the top of a lemon pie! Oh, I exaggerate, of course. One does with Victoria.

"I wonder if you *do* know as much as Punch knows," she remarked, thoughtfully exhaling a deep lungful of smoke. "Oh, I suppose so, though Alec had the idea that Punch might have taken it himself. Not to keep, of course," she added hastily, "but perhaps as a prank to teach his grandmother a lesson. Or to save it from being stolen by burglars."

Victoria went down to her nadir with me just then. I've never found it harder to keep up the appearance of friendliness.

"For that matter," I said, "I may have taken the thing myself. Gone over on crutches in my sleep...."

"That is possible," she interrupted, with a sudden look of interest. "Oh, not you. Punch! I don't *think* he ever has walked in his sleep. He may have done it this time, though. That necklace has been an obsession with him for days."

There was no denying, of course, that this was a possibility. But Victoria didn't pursue it.

"I'll tell you why I came," she went on, laying down her cigarette and coming a little more sharply into focus. "Alec is acting rather stupid about this and stubborn. He gets that from his mother, I guess. He's determined to make a hullabaloo about it. Send for detectives, question the servants, search everybody, and that sort of thing. Judy and I have done all we could to call him off, without getting anywhere. He feels his responsibility, he says, as the man of the family. All I could get him to agree to was to wait until he'd talked to you. He's in the dining-room now smoking with the men, but he's coming over to see you as soon as he can get away."

"And *you* want me to persuade him to do nothing," I said.

I didn't inflect it like a question. Cowardice that was, I'll admit. And Victoria assumed that I would do as she wished. It is an assumption she always makes with men, I think.

"Of course," she went on petulantly, "I don't know whether it will do any good. There'll be my mother-in-law to reckon with as soon as she comes out of the hypodermic Miss Digby gave her. I want Alec on our side, actively, you know, before that happens."

"Yes," I said faintly, "I see."

Then I rallied my courage. I admit it was the memory of what Punch had said—"I want the thief caught. I'm not afraid who it'll turn out to be"—which served as my trumpet call.

"Look here, Victoria. There may be a reason why I should try to persuade Alexander Corbin to let the necklace go and keep the theft dark, but I won't undertake it unless I know what the reason is."

She looked at me a little ruefully. "You never did like me very well," she remarked.

"I think I can fairly be counted one of your friends," I told her, "and I think I've understood pretty well some of your difficulties. I really want to help you now. But I can't step off in the dark. I want to know why the thing Alec proposes isn't the natural thing to do; the thing I'd do myself in the circumstances. He *has* got a responsibility in the matter, and I don't wonder that he feels it."

"Oh, I suppose so," she agreed.

I looked up at her and saw, to my astonishment, that there were tears in her eyes.

"You talk about my difficulties. You *don't* know them; not the beginning of them. I've been trying for the last ten years to give my children the sort of bringing up they deserve to have. It's the only thing I've cared anything about. That's true, whether you believe it or not. And I've been hampered and suspected and quarreled with all the time by that terrible old woman who's my mother-in-law.

"I suppose I've made mistakes. We all do. But between her and the children I've been driven half distracted. Not Punch. He's all right. But there have been times when I've been in despair about Judy."

"Isn't she pretty young to have been despaired about?" I protested.

"She ran away from school last fall," said Victoria. "I wonder if even *you* had heard about that? She simply disappeared for almost a month. There, I'm glad I told you. You'll have some idea...."

"Good heavens!" I broke in. "Didn't you hear from her in all that time? How did you know she hadn't been kidnapped—murdered?"

"I got a line from her every two or three days, post-marked from different places, saying she was all right and telling me not to worry."

"But how did she live?" I asked. "What had she to live on?"

"She earned it," Victoria said shortly. "You may be perfectly sure I haven't asked for details. But she's volunteered a few. I know she worked for a while as a waitress in a cheap lunch room."

"How did you get her back?"

"Oh, she'd had enough of it, I suppose. She wrote me that if I wanted her to come back she was ready to behave herself. I met her in New York. Found her in the Martha Washington Hotel, fitted her out with clothes, and took her, by a lucky chance, down to Belleair."

"What did she look like—when you found her, I mean?"

"She looked," Victoria said dryly, "as if she hadn't found liberty quite so jolly as she'd expected."

"What was the particular piece of luck about your choosing Belleair?"

"Why, Bruce was down there playing golf," she said. "And it just happened she got him. Of course if he'd known.... But there's no reason why he ever should. So now she's all right. She's marrying a man—an orphan, thank heaven!—who's well-bred and decently rich, and mad about her."

"Is she in love with him?" I asked.

"No," Victoria admitted, "I don't suppose she is. But she likes him, and she wants to marry him. She's going into it with her eyes open. And not under any pressure from me. I didn't urge it on her. Anyhow, that's *settled*. She's going to marry him day after tomorrow.

"Well, I'm not going to have her wedding spoiled by exploding a beastly thing like this in the middle of it."

"There's nothing beastly about getting robbed of a necklace," I said. "That can happen to anybody."

She flung out her hands in a gesture of uncontrollable exasperation. Then she pulled herself together.

"The first discovery a detective would make would be that Mrs Corbin is a morphine addict. That would be rather unsavory, wouldn't it?"

"She gets the stuff legitimately, doesn't she?" I commented. "Nobody as old and rich as that could be reduced to trafficking with a peddler."

"Oh, yes," she admitted. "Doctor Parkinson prescribes it for her. But isn't that bad enough? Bruce would hate it—just the notoriety—worse than anybody I know. Things like that simply don't happen in his family. He'd think less of Judy if it happened in hers."

She paused a moment; then went on with a rush. "If this meant the actual loss of the necklace itself, I'd let it go; let the thief make what he could out of it—rather than turn Judy's wedding into a beastly dime novel of a detective story. Have it smeared all over the front pages of the newspapers. Isn't that reason enough why Alec shouldn't tell the world with a bang what's happened?"

She could hardly have been aware of what she had said, for she started when I quoted her own words back at her.

"You said just now that even if it really meant the loss of the necklace you'd let it go. Do you mean that it doesn't mean that?"

She took her time before answering. "I'm absolutely sure it doesn't," she said.

"Do you *know* where the necklace is now, Victoria?"

"No," she said hotly, "of course I don't. Not exactly. But I'm absolutely sure that it's all right."

"How about Judy?" I asked. "Does she agree with you, genuinely, that it's best to do nothing about it?"

Victoria gave me a rather dry smile. "Judy does," she said. "You may be perfectly sure of that. Call her up on the phone if you like and ask her."

"No," I said. "I'll take your word for it. And I'll do what I can to bring Alexander around to your way of thinking."

She nodded and got up to go, without, I'm glad to say, embarrassing me by any overwhelming manifestations of gratitude. I wasn't enthusiastic over what I'd let myself in for.

I didn't believe Victoria was as sure as she pretended to be that the necklace would turn up all right. The start of interest she had betrayed over the idea that Punch might have taken it while walking in his sleep had looked genuine, and Victoria never was much of an actress. If it was genuine, it revealed two things. First, that she hadn't carried off the necklace herself on that hurried trip to town yesterday, and second, that she didn't know who had taken it. All she had was a theory, but it must be one in which she felt a good deal of confidence.

Whom could that theory concern? It seemed to narrow itself down to Judy. A reduction to absurdity, of course. Why should Judy steal the necklace which her grandmother meant to give her for a wedding present? And yet, why had Judy faked a sprained ankle? Why had she asked her brother whether he'd be on her side whatever she did? Why had she laughed in that queer way when she saw the empty box from which the necklace had been taken?

My belief in the child's honor, in her essential straightness, was impregnable. It had not been in the least shaken by Victoria's account of her escapade last fall, the running away from the school she had hated—earning her own living by being a waitress in a quick lunch. Good lord!

I could understand her doing that, though. What was harder to understand was her sudden surrender. It wasn't like Judy to come to heel just because she'd found that liberty wasn't quite what it was cracked up to be. Something worse than that must have happened to her. Whatever had happened, though, even if she'd got involved in devious ways, I was sure they weren't of her seeking. I felt about this present business much as Punch did. I wanted the thief caught; the air, so sultry with mystery and suspicion, cleared by a good fresh wind.

And yet I had just given Victoria my promise to do what I could to help hush things up. Why the devil had I done that? Well, I knew why. It was because, when she had said that her children were all in the world that she really cared anything about, I had believed she was telling the truth. All the same I didn't relish the prospect of my talk with Alexander Corbin.

That, however, came off better than I had anticipated. I found I liked him, just as Punch had done. And he showed no trace of the stubbornness of which Victoria had accused him. He seemed to me extraordinarily open-minded, and he carried the virtue of candor further than I'd have been able to do myself, I think, in similar circumstances.

I remembered him faintly, as one would remember the younger brother of a boyhood friend, and by way of putting some feeling of cordiality into my greeting, I told him so, without the qualifications.

"That's nice of you," he said. "But you wouldn't have recognized me if you'd met me on the street."

"No," I admitted, "I don't suppose I should."

"Well, there you are!" he said. "I doubt if anybody would. I'm all but a total stranger. And I find myself in the middle of a family snarl like this. I come on here for my niece's wedding, and within twenty-four hours a highly portable piece of my mother's property, worth perhaps a hundred thousand dollars, disappears."

"Good God!" I cried. "You aren't trying to tell me that any one suspects *you* of having taken it?"

"That's very polite of you," he remarked kindly, "but I don't see why they shouldn't. It's evident that Victoria and Judy both regard it as an inside job of some sort. And surely I've a more obvious motive, as they say in detective stories, for taking it than any one else in the family. I quarreled with my mother pretty near thirty years ago; I've come home at last to make it up; I find her so shaken by age and—infirmity that it's very doubtful if any new will she made now would hold water,—and I steal the necklace by way of getting my share of the estate.

"It's all rot, of course, but that's how it looks. What I'd like to do is to put a cordon around the house and have everybody in it searched, beginning with me and Applebury's maiden aunts. I want it found, if it involves tearing the plaster off the walls. Of course it isn't possible to go to such lengths as that, but it seems as if one might do something.

"Yet here's Victoria pleading with me to let it ride; not turn a hand nor say a word. She seems to think she knows where it is, or at all events, that it will turn up. Well, that's all right if she's got the correct hunch. But suppose she hasn't? I'll feel uncommonly flat facing my mother tomorrow when she comes out of the effect of the stuff they've given her, if I have to tell her that the necklace hasn't been heard from, and that I've done nothing toward recovering it."

"I'm not sure," I said, "that you haven't done the best thing possible toward recovering it."

He looked at me with a stare of surprise. "You mean by doing nothing, by saying nothing?" he asked. "That's what you must mean, of course, because that's all I've done. But I'm not sure that I see how you figure it out. Effect of suspense and uncertainty—that sort of thing? Psychology getting in its deadly work?"

"Something like that," I said.

"Well, it won't, and I'll tell you why. A thing like that can't be kept dark. It's known already—half known. Things like that get passed around. I could feel it crackling all around the dinner table tonight. By morning everybody in the house will know that something's happened. And Victoria might as well have let me call the police in the first place."

"No," I insisted. "There's a difference between knowing a thing that's admitted and knowing a thing that's not admitted. Society—with a big S— lives on that difference. We never call anybody a liar. We go on acting as if we believed the official version of things until the facts fairly stare us down."

He laughed. "That statement is true," he said, "and it's equally true of the Moro chieftains in the island of Mindanao."

"All right," I said. "Now consider this. There are three sorts of persons in that house: family, guests and servants. They're all going to stay until after the wedding, day after tomorrow. There's no reason why anybody should leave, at least, and if anybody does, on whatever pretext, he'll be under heavy suspicion. But it's not likely that the person who took the necklace will try to leave. The hullabaloo and the breaking up of the party is very likely just what he's hoping for. But nothing happens. Nothing's said. And the inference from that is that someone's been found out. That we know and therefore we can afford to wait. So there's a pretty good chance that the thief, so to speak, will take his first opportunity to restore the necklace."

"That's ingenious," he was polite enough to say. "But I confess the strong-arm method appeals to me rather more."

"It can't be applied," I said. "A search is no good unless you search everybody."

"That's what I want," he insisted. "That's exactly what I mean. Everybody."

"Including your mother?" I asked.

Again I encountered his quick intense stare. It wasn't hostile, though. He was thinking, hard.

"You're right," he said. "That can't be done."

He seemed to be coming around all right by himself, so I let him alone. There was a ruminative silence between us for a while.

"That's a nice little niece of mine," he said at last. "Hard to realize she's getting married, though. I wish I knew her better."

"What do you think of her young man?" I asked.

"Oh, a perfectly sound fellow, I think," he said, without enthusiasm. "No mistaking his type. He's what he is, plain as a flagstaff. Great on discipline and exercise. Plays a very good game of bridge and takes it as seriously as he does the Constitution of the United States. He'll have a thick neck by the time he's forty, and be one of the pillars of an intensely respectable club. Seems like rather a sledge-hammer, though, for little Judy."

"Is that at all the way she feels, do you think?" I asked.

He was properly non-committal about that. "Oh, don't ask me," he said. "The etiquette is so different from what it was in my day. Then a young couple like that would have played up—held hands, slunk off by themselves whenever they got a chance. I've hardly seen these two together since he got here. That's the modern manner, I suppose."

I'd been thinking over what Punch had told me of the arrival of the guests. There had been nothing unnatural about Judy's greeting of her fiancé or of the others who came down from the station in the same car with him.

Punch had spoken of hearing her laugh two or three times after he'd taken his sentry post on the davenport up-stairs. Whatever had happened to her had happened after that.

"Is there anybody in the crowd that came down on the special car," I asked, "anybody who arrived at The Oaks later than Bruce did, who has—well, attracted your attention in any way? Anybody who seemed to have any special effect on Judy?"

For the third time he turned upon me that intense stare of his.

"No," he said, "I can't say there is. I don't know why you asked me that, but I'll tell you this. I happened to be looking at her—it's the natural thing to do—and I saw her face change. I couldn't say now whether it was with pleasure or the reverse. She was looking past me. Then she turned with a sort of gasp, and bolted into the house. It must have been just then that she hurt her ankle. I know I turned around to try to see who or what she'd been looking at, but I didn't make anything of it. It was something, though, or somebody."

I nodded. "That's it," I said. "There's something behind, that Judy and her mother know more about than we do. Wheels within wheels, you know."

"All right," he said, getting up with a rueful sort of laugh, "I won't throw a monkey-wrench into the machinery just yet. We'll let another day go by and see what happens. But if nothing does happen within the next twenty-four hours, I think it will be a case for the police."

CHAPTER V

THE LEGS OF A SUIT OF PAJAMAS

Punch didn't want to be sent to bed, so he was adroitly evading his mother's notice, flitting about the edges of the evening's gaiety and lingering in the shadows. It was a warm windless evening. It would be stuffy in his little room on the top floor and he was feeling wide awake and rather restless. But out-of-doors, in the verandas and on the lawn, it was nice. The moon was dead full, hanging, an undisputed dignitary, in the cloudless sky. Not so exciting as when it went sailing through a scud of flying clouds, but he didn't crave excitement just now. He'd had enough.

They were dancing in the big west drawing-room—some of them were. Some of them seemed to share—though it couldn't be from the fear of being sent to bed—his own preference for the shadows. In a sort of glade down at the bottom of the lawn, so far away that the music must almost have been inaudible, one pair were dancing, barefoot, Punch believed. There'd been some talk of what fun it would be, and Judy had applauded the idea, though she herself wasn't dancing, of course, because of her ankle.

She was permanently established in a long chair in the corner of the veranda, holding a sort of court between dances, and always with one man or another beside her when the music played. She adored dancing, Punch knew, and he wondered a little that she didn't permit her ankle to get better.

Bruce Applebury danced indefatigably. He always came back with his partner and sat beside Judy during the intermissions. But Punch had heard Judy tell him it was his duty to make the rounds of at least all the brides-maids, so he didn't sit out many dances with her.

Punch was beginning to feel a little like a ghost. The mixture of cold moonlight with the music and the odor of a great thicket of lilac bushes in bloom at the corner of the house, was distilling a sort of melancholy in him, when the voice of the one he had privately ticketed as the nice bridesmaid roused him from the trance into which he was drifting.

"Oh, but I've promised this dance to Punch," he heard her say to the man who, with his hand on her arm, was trying to lead her down from the veranda to the lawn.

He'd approached them unconsciously in his irregular orbit—Judy was the center of it—but on hearing this, he stopped before her and made her his best bow. The man, with a laugh, relinquished her arm, said he'd come back for the next, and strolled away, lighting a cigarette.

Punch didn't know the girl's name; their acquaintance had begun in a spontaneous exchange of smiles at the tennis court, and they'd had a lot of fun together in the pool.

"I *can* dance," he said, a little doubtfully, when they were left alone, "but I'm not sure that mother doesn't think I've gone to bed."

The girl laughed and laid her hand on his arm. "We'll go for a little walk instead then," she decided.

She was a nice girl, and Punch didn't think she'd make the opening remark which some of the others, earlier in the day, had devastated him with, "Won't you miss Judy horribly when she's married?"

His confidence was justified. She didn't. She talked about sensible things: swimming strokes, and how it felt the first time you tried a high dive; the probable delights of owning a motorcycle, and so on. Eventually they got around to talking about the pleasures of not traveling in Europe and the advantages of being an American.

When they heard the music stop, he said, with real regret, "I suppose if you're promised for the next dance I'd better take you back." After a ripple of applause they heard the dance go on again, but now they were strolling back toward the house.

"I envy Judy," she said suddenly. "I wish I had a nice young brother of my own."

"If you did," Punch blurted out, "you'd probably just go and get married."

She withdrew her hand from his arm, where it had rested quite comfortably all the while. He needed both his hands just then, for his eyes were threatening him with disaster. She put her arm across his shoulders and for a moment held him tight. Then she let him go, and walked on.

"It's funny how black the shadows are in the moonlight," she said. "You can't see a thing. Do you know yet where you're going to college?"

She *was* a nice girl.

They came up into the veranda just as the dance was coming to an end— really this time. The man she had left was waiting there to claim her, and Punch turned for a look at Judy. He had an idea that he might sit out the next dance with her.

She happened, just then, to be alone. A moment earlier, Punch was sure, a man had been standing before her, bending over. Now he was gone, and Judy was holding something in her hand. A letter, or what looked like it.

Not just a scrap of a note, for when she tried to fold it small it offered some resistance.

This movement seemed half frightened, although this didn't exactly describe the look that was in her face. She started to tuck the thing down inside her dress, suddenly desisted and, with an exasperated laugh, snatched it out again. She glanced around, helplessly at a loss. Then her hand darted out to a narrow-necked Chinese vase which stood on the table beside her, and she pushed her letter down inside. It wouldn't be very easy to get out again, Punch reflected, for the hastily folded paper would spring apart.

The next moment Bruce Applebury came out through the open French window from the drawing-room and sat down beside her.

"Just on the minute," she remarked to him. "Like a man in a play."

Punch stood rooted where he was. He wouldn't have gone to her even if Bruce Applebury hadn't come out. The fog of trouble which the nice bridesmaid had for the while dissipated stole again over his spirit.

He didn't know who the man was who had given Judy the letter—except, of course, that it wasn't Bruce. He'd barely glimpsed him out of the corner of his eye. There was something secret and hasty about the whole episode that didn't go with his idea of Judy. What he hated worst about it was the look in her face that disputed with the fright in it.

He was sunk so deep in a brown study that his mother caught him without difficulty and sent him to bed.

But it wasn't so easy to send him to sleep. The music went on and on, floating in through his open window, nagging his jangled nerves. It was punctuated, too, by disconcerting little fragments of talk coming up astonishingly clear now and then from the strollers on the lawn. Nothing that meant anything; just broken phrases, exclamations, giggles. It annoyed him that people could be so horribly silly.

He must have drifted off, though, at last, for he sat up suddenly in bed, bolt awake from an unreasonably unpleasant dream. The party must be over, and everybody gone to bed, for the house was silent, except, he noted with disgust, for the grumble of conversation that was going on in the adjoining bedroom. Bill Grant's it was, and he imagined he identified the other voice, that was doing most of the talking, as Bruce Applebury's. He couldn't hear what they were saying. He was afraid though that if they talked any louder, he might hear.

He lay down again and turned and tossed. No hope of getting asleep till they stopped. Finally, in desperation he got up, padded softly out through the billiard room to a near-by bathroom, got himself a drink and splashed his hot face with cold water. This refreshed him somewhat, but he didn't want to go back to his room. The big davenport in the hall, one flight down, occurred to him as a quieter, and perhaps cooler, place to sleep. He wouldn't need any covers. It was too hot a night. So with infinite precautions against noise he stole down there. He'd meant to sleep there anyway if the necklace had not already been stolen.

It wasn't very dark down there in the second-floor hall. It had two big windows at one end and an enormous one above the stair-landing at the other. And the big moon still had everything her own way in the cloudless sky.

In spite of his precautions against making any noise, he did make one. In the process of disposing the pillows on the davenport, he dropped one on the floor with a plop.

A moment or two later Judy's door opened, and she asked, in a clear, penetrating whisper, "Who's that?"

"I dropped a pillow," he said. "I didn't mean to disturb you."

"You!" she said.

She came over to the davenport and stood looking down at him. She had on the same orange-colored kimono that she'd worn when she went to her grandmother's room before dinner.

"What are you doing down here?" she asked. "Still keeping watch?"

"It was stuffy up in my room," he explained, "and I couldn't sleep."

She gave a little shiver, not with cold, and sat down beside where he lay.

"I can't sleep either," she told him. "It's beastly. Punch, I tell you what let's do. Let's go out for a ride on bicycles. There's another one besides yours up in the old stable. You go ahead and get them, and I'll meet you here by the corner of the veranda."

If he'd been feeling just right about Judy he'd have taken the thing as a lark and gone, but he didn't feel right. Her mention of the corner of the veranda reminded him of something.

"I don't want to go up-stairs and get dressed," he objected. "There were some people talking up there when I came down."

She seemed concerned by that and asked him quickly, "Who?"

"I don't know," he told her. "They were in Bill Grant's room."

She glanced sharply in the direction of the stairs as if she thought she'd heard something, but decided she hadn't.

"You don't have to dress," she pleaded. "Pajamas are all right, and I'll lend you a pair of my sneakers."

"The whole house is locked up tight," he objected. "We'd probably set off the burglar alarm if we tried to open a door or a window down-stairs."

"We can go out my window, can't we?"

That made the thing seem more fun, and he all but yielded; indeed he had moved to get up from the davenport, when he noticed something.

"You've started to dress already, Judy," he said.

"Shirt and bloomers," she admitted. "Yes, I was going out anyway. I was getting ready to when I heard you drop that pillow. I've left something I want, down on the veranda."

"That letter?" he asked.

There was a breathless sort of silence between them.

At last she said, "Don't you care, Punch. You'll understand some day, maybe."

He'd have gone with her then if he'd felt sure she wanted him, sure that the proposal of a ride with him hadn't been a mere pretext of hers for an opportunity to recover her letter while he was up at the stable getting out the bicycles. It was with a very sore spirit that he lay down on the davenport again and let her go back to her own room and close the door after her without a word.

He lay there straining his ears for a sound from her, but she must have been moving about as quietly as a ghost for he heard nothing. Perhaps he'd be able to hear her when she came in though, and she'd turn on the light, wouldn't she, to read her letter by?

But still there was nothing. The silence in the big house remained unbroken.

He stood it as long as he could; then went to Judy's door, opened it and after a glance about the deserted room, left it open. He'd know, now, when she came back, anyhow.

After that once more he fell asleep, only to be wakened as before by a dream, or so he supposed at the moment, though he realized afterward that the soft closing of a door might have done it. He sat up, and now he heard footsteps shuffling along in felt slippers, and turning he saw a man in pajamas crossing the hall.

There was more light than ever now. The moon shone slantwise through the great window on the landing and threw a brightly lighted patch upon the floor. As the legs of these pajamas crossed this patch he saw them very plainly. They were gray, or lavender, or perhaps a washed-out blue, and there was a triangular tear, such as might happen from getting caught on a nail, in one of them. The rest of the man he couldn't see so well, and in a moment he was nothing but a shadowed silhouette.

Punch almost spoke to him automatically, but checked himself with the reflection that by doing so he'd give some slightly embarrassed guest on his way to the bathroom a horrible start.

The next moment he sat up straighter and held his breath. The man didn't turn into the bathroom. He went straight on up-stairs. That was strange. Why should a guest who slept on this floor go up-stairs in the middle of the night? Or if his room were up there, why had he come down?

The boy was rather frightened now, and the realization that he was made it a point of honor with him to investigate the mystery if he could. So softly and swiftly he stole up-stairs too, alert for the sound of a closing door or glimpse of a streak of light under one of them. There wasn't a sound, and the blackness up here in the billiard room was all but complete. Was somebody lurking there, waiting? Someone who had heard his following footsteps?

He stood still, overcoming a panicky impulse of flight. He at last mustered his courage—really considerable, it seems to me—to the point of moving over to the switch and turning on the light in the tin-shaded chandelier over the table. The room was empty. The mystery remained unsolved.

Well, he had done all he could anyhow, and he turned off the light again and stole down-stairs.

He now went into Judy's room and glanced around. No, she hadn't come back yet. She must have gone on that bicycle ride after all. It must be horribly late. He carried her watch from the night-table to the window. After three. He stole back to his uneasy bed on the davenport.

He wasn't yet quite at the end of his night's adventures. He sprang up again almost before he'd had time to lie down. His grandmother's door was opening. Somebody with an electric torch was coming out.

"Who's that?" he asked sharply.

The figure gave a violent start. It was Miss Digby in her old plum-colored bathrobe.

"Punch!" she cried, "what are you doing here?"

"Trying to get a night's sleep," he said. "What's happened? Is anything wrong with grandmother?"

"No," Miss Digby said. "I was waked up a few minutes ago by hearing this door shut. I've been frightened pretty near out of my wits. I wish you wouldn't go poking around the house in the middle of the night."

He didn't tell her he hadn't shut a door. The only thing on his mind was Judy's door standing open. Old Digs mustn't go in there and find that she was gone. So he told her he wouldn't poke around any more, and, glad to be rid of her so easily, went back to the davenport.

CHAPTER VI

REWARD OF MERIT

Punch told me he didn't know when it happened; whether he dreamed it, or whether it broke over him as he was falling asleep or just in the moment of his waking up.

He lay awake for ever so long after promising Miss Digby he wouldn't go poking around any more, worrying because Judy didn't come back; wondering what could be in the letter she was willing to risk so much to get; speculating over the mysterious errand of the man in the gray pajamas. But all these thoughts got him nowhere. His mind, so he described it, was just playing leap frog with itself. He saw the sky turn gray, and then pink.

Finally, when it was broad day, he fell asleep. And the next thing he knew, Miss Digby was shaking him by the shoulder, telling him it was half past eight and he'd really better go up to his room and dress.

His first thought was of Judy's door, and his first glance showed him that it was shut. But this, he instantly perceived, didn't mean anything. The servants must have been up for at least an hour. The chambermaid, seeing Judy's room empty, would have assumed she'd gone for an early ride, made up her room and closed the door after her. However, it was good as far as it went. Judy might be in there, sound asleep in bed. Probably was.

Miss Digby gave his shoulder another shake. "Punch, you're still half asleep," she insisted. "Get up."

Then he sat up, blinking at her, and realized all in an instant, or thought he did, that he knew the whole thing. The puzzle had worked.

"Have you found them yet?" he asked.

"Found what?" she demanded impatiently.

He must still have looked to her like a sleepy little boy, for she added, "Wake up!"

"I'm awake now, all right," he told her. "Have you found the pearls—the necklace—in grandmother's room?"

"If you aren't half asleep, you're out of your head!" she told him sharply. "How should I find them? They were stolen. Have you forgotten? Last night before dinner."

"Sure, they were stolen," he agreed. "They've been brought back. A man brought them back last night. That's what you heard. Him shutting the door just as he was going out."

She went rather white at that and stood staring at him. It must have been, of course, to that respectable spinster, a perfectly horrifying idea that any man had invaded the room where she was sleeping, let alone a thief.

"If you're joking," she went on, gathering herself together, "all I can say is that it's extremely bad taste."

"I'm not joking," he told her. "Listen. Don't you remember coming out last night and telling me you'd heard a door shut. I hadn't shut any door—but I'd seen the man."

"You'd seen a *man*! Going into that room?"

"No, of course not. If I'd have seen him going into that room, I'd have done something about it. I saw him going along the hall in pajamas. I thought he was going to the bathroom, there at the foot of the stairs.

"Instead of doing that he went up the stairs, and I thought it was funny, because why should a man on this floor go up-stairs in the middle of the night? So I followed him up to see who he was and where he went. I didn't see him at all, after he'd turned the corner at the landing. So I came down again. And then you came out and said you had heard a door shut.

"I didn't figure it out at the time, but it's plain enough now. He's the man who stole the necklace. But he'd made up his mind that he wasn't going to get away with it, so he brought it back. You'll find it's in there."

She was shaken all right, but still a long way from being convinced.

"I think you're talking perfectly crazy nonsense," she declared. "Punch, aren't you making it up—about the man in pajamas?"

"Do you think I'd joke about a thing like that?" he demanded hotly. "The necklace is there, I tell you. I'll bet anything it is. Is grandmother awake yet?"

"No, she's still sleeping I think."

"That must have been some hypodermic you gave her last night," Punch commented. "Come along then; let's look."

Still with a strong air of protest, she followed him to the old woman's sitting-room. Punch darted across to the safe.

"That's locked," Miss Digby commented. "Mr. Alexander Corbin locked it last night."

Punch tried the handle and found she was right.

"He'd have put it in there if he could," he said reflectively. "But it wouldn't have been worth the risk of stopping to unlock it, with you right here. So he's left it somewhere around the room. It's like I-Spy," he commented, with a little laugh.

He stood still looking about. Presently his eye fell on the long morocco covered box lying disregarded and unvalued on the big table in the middle of the room.

"That's where it is, of course," he said. "Look and see."

Where she stood it was almost under her hand. With trembling fingers she pressed the spring and the lid flew open. There the necklace was, gleaming, creamy and wonderful, under the shadow of the box lid.

Miss Digby gasped and stood for a moment clinging to the edge of the table for support. Then, to Punch's utter consternation, she turned upon him.

"Punch," she cried, "how could you! How *could* you! Do you hate me as much as that?"

"How could I what?" he asked, from the depths of a profound bewilderment.

She dropped into his grandmother's big chair and broke into a passionate fit of weeping.

"I knew they'd think I'd taken it. I'm the one who could. Your grandmother leaves the safe open half the time, and sometimes, when she can't remember the combination, I have to unlock it for her. And then you take it—for a joke, I suppose—and bring it back, after I've been in torture for hours and hours, and make me find it."

"Nobody suspected you, Digs," he told her. "Nobody could have. But I didn't take it, and I didn't bring it back."

He stood there for a few miserable minutes, helplessly at a loss. Then he said, "Well, I guess I'd better go and tell mother they're back." With that he left the room.

He didn't, however, go straight to his mother with the news. He sat down for a while first, feeling rather weak in the legs, on the davenport.

Old Digs' accusation disturbed him, but not profoundly. Uncle Alec would probably think as Miss Digby did, that he'd taken the necklace for a joke, and it would be pretty hard to convince him to the contrary. Really, no one could be blamed for regarding his story of the man in the pajamas as fishy.

But his mother and Judy couldn't think that, or wouldn't be likely to, because they thought they knew who the thief was. Otherwise they wouldn't so strongly have opposed calling in the police.

That letter Judy had got last evening on the veranda probably had contained a full confession of what she'd suspected. She'd had to hide it before she had time to read it because she'd seen Bruce coming out of the drawing-room, and he might have asked her about it. Why she hadn't hidden it in her dress as she'd started to do, he couldn't make out. Probably for the minute she'd just lost her head. But having shoved it down into that Chinese vase, she'd have some trouble getting it out again, and she'd have to be by herself in order to do it. And of course she had to get it back unless she wanted to run the risk that someone else would find it.

This did pretty well, although it wasn't a wholly satisfactory explanation. It didn't cover all the ground. It didn't explain why Judy hadn't climbed back into her window again within ten minutes after the time she'd climbed out of it.

He was under an almost overmastering impulse to go into her room now, see if she was there, and if she was, tell her about the recovery of the necklace before he told even his mother. He decided he mustn't do it. Suppose she weren't there? Then he'd have to tell his mother that she was gone. He'd be asked whether he knew anything about her flight and he couldn't be sure that loyalty to Judy would permit him to tell what he knew.

He'd better go to his mother first. Then perhaps he wouldn't be asked any questions about his sister. After all, it was good news he was bringing. The necklace had been restored, and it wouldn't be necessary to tell anybody, beyond those who already knew, that it had ever disappeared.

He knocked on his mother's door and she told him, rather quickly, to come in. She was sitting up in bed, her breakfast tray on her lap, the morning mail beside her.

"You oughtn't to be wandering all over the house at this time of day in your pajamas," she told him—good-naturedly enough, though. "Why don't you go up and get dressed?"

"I've been having quite a night of it," he said. "But it's all right now. Mother, the necklace is back!"

Then he stood staring at her, speechless, utterly appalled, for her face—lips and all—had turned gray.

"Back!" she said. "What do you mean?" And then like the crack of a whip, "Where is it? Who's got it?"

"D—Digs," he managed to say. "It's—it's in grandmother's room. In the box where she kept it. On her table."

"Digs found it, did she?" Victoria asked.

"Yes," Punch said, "she found it, but—but I told her that was where it would be."

"Oh God!" Victoria cried out.

She sprang out of bed, pulled her dressing-gown around her and, without waiting for slippers, darted toward the door. Then she came back, and rummaging furiously among her letters in the morning's mail found one which she took with her.

She went straight across the hall with it to Judy's room, and Punch followed right at her heels. He was afraid she'd send him back, but she didn't seem to know he was there.

cape to The Oaks until dinner time tonight—that I didn't look forward much to six or eight hours of the ancient man's undiluted society.

I passed a restless unpleasant sort of morning, and by eleven o'clock I was feeling sorry for myself. Punch hadn't turned up for his morning call. I was mindful, too, of Judy's promise to come and give me a look at Bruce Applebury. Unless they came early, before old Mr. Ethelbert Smith arrived, I shouldn't have much chance for a real visit with them.

They hadn't come, though, nor had I received any word of any sort from The Oaks, when, at a little after eleven, Victoria delivered her guest at my door. On hearing the car drive up I'd sent out Donovan, my nurse, to help fetch the old gentleman inside, and I'm afraid I betrayed my surprise with an unmannerly stare when there came in at her heels a very tall old man, slender and straight as a lance, as he stood erect after the rather ceremonious bow he had made when he ushered Victoria into my doorway.

Anything more unlike the image of senile decay which she had prepared me for, it would be hard to imagine. He was old, to be sure, very old, perhaps, for his lean clean-shaven face was deeply lined and his short white hair was, no doubt, thinner than it once had been. He looked a little like the picture of Oliver Wendell Holmes. Not Mr. Justice Holmes—his father. His dark eyes had a twinkle of ironic amusement in them, which may have been due merely to the astonishment I had momentarily exhibited at sight of him, or may have been due to something else.

Victoria introduced us rather breathlessly and then, cutting across our politely reciprocal murmurs, said, "I really can't stop a minute. If you knew what things were like at the house.... You'll both excuse me, won't you? And we'll all see you at dinner; it's at eight, you know."

With that she was gone, so hastily that she almost collided in the entry with the chauffeur who was bringing in Mr. Smith's bags.

"There's a certain economy about Victoria's method," he remarked in a tone of dry amusement. He added instantly, with the friendliest concern, "Oh, don't let me keep you on your crutches." He waved me back to my couch, and to make it easier for me to obey the gracious gesture, he promptly seated himself in a near-by chair.

"I'm afraid she's rather foisted me upon you," he went on, "under the pretext that she can't make me comfortable in the other house. I don't know what she thinks I want. I'm an old campaigner, and not an exigent person at all, so you're not to allow me to weigh upon your conscience or your spirits. Presently your man shall show me where my room is, and then you're to trust me to make myself comfortable."

He left me with something to think about after these suggestions had been carried out. Whatever reason Victoria might have had for not wanting Mr. Ethelbert Smith at The Oaks, it was not the reason she had given me.

The man would have been a social asset at any house party. I felt sure that he would have enjoyed the jolly confusion generated by a crowd of high-spirited young people as well as anybody. And I believed Victoria knew it perfectly well. They seemed, at least, to be pretty well acquainted. His characterization of her high-handed ways as "economy of method" showed that.

He'd seemed a little surprised at my asking him if he'd just returned from Paris.

"Oh, no," he said. "I retired from business several years ago and when I did that I came home. I do a little work now and then—for Lloyds, mostly—just to keep from getting rusty, and by way of having leisure to enjoy. A man with no occupation, you know," he remarked, "has no leisure. He's kept busy all the time looking for something to do."

I laughed at that, tapped my stone leg and told him I agreed with him heartily.

It may have been this expression of my own weariness of doing nothing which led him, when he came down-stairs again a little later, coolly clad in mohair, to make a suggestion which produced some unexpected results.

"I was thinking of going out for a stroll," he said, "but why don't you come with me? That wheel-chair of yours looks seaworthy. I saw a pleasant little summer-house up on the hill, beyond your ruins. Couldn't Donovan wheel you up there, with a little help perhaps from me? You'd enjoy a change and a new view, and, I should think, a certain amount of exercise."

It was a perfectly practicable idea, as well as an attractive one, so we carried it out at once. I wondered a little that I hadn't thought of it myself days ago. He carried my field-glasses along to amuse himself with and I was munitioned with a book, so that he might feel at liberty to stroll off and leave me if the humor took him. This, after a period of pleasant chat about nothing in particular, is what he did.

The summer-house is nothing much but a conical roof supported by rustic trellised poles, open at all sides to the breeze, and though these are more or less overgrown with vines, it still commands a pretty wide prospect all around the hill. I turned my back on the melancholy ruin of my house and faced down the path by which we had come, the cottage in the middle of my view with the road to The Oaks winding down the valley.

I sat there contentedly enough for quite a while, ruminating and hardly more than half awake. The mysteries connected with old Mrs. Corbin's necklace were still mysterious to me, to be sure, but since the thing had been returned, my interest in it was largely academic. I hadn't, you are to remember, seen Punch that morning.

I was mildly curious about my guest. I wondered what the business had been that had kept him living in Paris so many years. He hadn't volunteered to tell me, and of course I hadn't asked. And what was the sort of work that he did occasionally for Lloyds? Since they write every conceivable kind of insurance, the name didn't tell me much.

I was aroused suddenly by becoming aware that I was going to have visitors. I can't say how, because I can't remember having heard their footsteps or their voices. My back was to the entrance, so I wheeled my chair around to see who it was.

Judy and her young man! She'd remembered her promise after all. They were almost upon me. She was holding out her hand to lead him inside.

"Here we are," she said to him.

One sees so quickly and so much, and it takes so long to tell! I had time to take him in from head to foot and to reflect that I liked him better, judging merely from his looks, than Punch or Alec Corbin, or even Judy herself had led me to believe I should. I had time to observe a deep sober preoccupation in both their faces; to see that he drew breath to speak, and to guess that he was going to say nothing but just her name.

And then suddenly I cried out, heartily and rather loudly, "Hello!" for I had also had time to realize that I must make my presence known at once.

They hadn't come to see me. They couldn't have expected to find me here unless they'd been to the cottage first, and if they'd done that they'd have been fairly in my field of vision all the way up.

They both started galvanically at my voice. Then the man scowled in my direction. No kindlier word will do for it; it was a black scowl and nothing else. I think Judy said something admonitory to him under her breath.

I realized, somehow, even in that moment of profound misunderstanding, that what I saw wasn't the mere vexation of a pair of lovers who had found already appropriated the retreat they'd intended for their love-making.

Judy came in at once, a curiously complicated look in her face—affection for me was a part of it—and gave me a brief kiss, expressive more than anything else of apology for their bad manners the moment before. She walked without a trace of a limp. Evidently she'd allowed her ankle to get well.

"It's perfectly great up here, isn't it?" she said.

"It's great now that you've come and brought Bruce Applebury to make that call you promised," I said, and held out a welcoming hand to him on the words.

He didn't come forward to take it, but remained as if rooted in the entrance to the summer-house. If ever I saw consternation written plain upon an open countenance, I saw it then.

Judy patted my shoulder encouragingly, as one might pat a horse that was going to shy.

"All wrong!" she said. "All wrong! We didn't come up here to see you. We came because we had something to talk about and I said I knew a good, safely deserted place where we could do it. And this isn't Bruce, you know. Bruce has gone to town on an errand. This is his cousin, Bill Grant."

She must have felt me give the start she'd been expecting. "Shake hands, you two," she commanded curtly.

I felt she meant it, somehow, as a guarantee, and held out my hand again, and this time he came forward and took it, but still without a word. Then he sat down heavily on the circular seat that ran around the place. His face was shining with sweat, and he got out his handkerchief and mopped it.

"You're out of condition, Bill," Judy remarked. "This life of crime is too much for you."

She sat down herself in a big hickory chair, straightened out her legs in front of her and looked thoughtfully at her feet. I take no blame for the ensuing silence. I can't think yet of anything I could have said.

Judy finally broke it. "After all," she said, looking up at Bill, "I don't know why not. Since he's here, maybe it's providential."

She turned to me. "You like to hear long stories, don't you? Stories of people's lives, their terrible pasts and all that? Do you want me to tell you one?"

She had startled her companion, I could see, but it wasn't, I thought, as if he meant to try to dissuade her.

"Go ahead and tell it," I said.

But before she had time to say another word, there were some more footsteps; jaunty footsteps, if that's a fair way to describe them. Judy's eyes widened as she listened. Bill Grant had sprung erect.

"It's Mr. Ethelbert Smith," I said swiftly. "He's staying with me, you know."

"Oh, damn!" whispered Judy. Then with a swoop she flew to meet him.

"Why, Judy!" I heard him cry. "This is delightful!"

"Isn't it?" she agreed. "But," she went on, reaching around for Bill Grant and hauling him out to be introduced, "this is not the blushing bridegroom; he's the next best man. Mr. Smith, Mr. Grant. Bruce's cousin, you know. Bruce had to go to town on an errand, so we're"—she waved a hand toward the grassy slope—"making hay."

"I can't blame either of you," he said gallantly, with a look of frank admiration from one to the other. "A much more respectable occupation than mine has been. I've been up there in the woods"—he patted my field-glasses—"spying upon the innocent domesticities of little birds."

There were no more silences after that. We all talked volubly and nobody really said anything. There wasn't a word about the necklace.

I wondered uneasily whether old Mr. Smith wasn't noticing something unnaturally vacuous about our talk. Certainly for an old family friend he was showing very little curiosity. He wasn't asking a question. Had he seen anything queer through those damned field-glasses of mine?

I kicked that question out of my mind with the contempt it deserved. Judy wasn't like that, anyhow. The great wonder, what the story was which she'd seemed to be on the point of telling me, I simply didn't dare let my mind dwell upon. That would have to wait.

It was mainly a relief, though my feelings were somewhat mixed, when Judy said, with a queer flicker of a smile at me, "Well, we must be going along. This is going to be a busy day," and took her "next best man" away with her.

They went, not down the path toward my cottage, but back by the way they had come.

CHAPTER VIII

EXPERT CONSIDERATION

I was afraid after they'd gone that old Mr. Smith would begin asking embarrassing questions, but his curiosity, if he had any, was under perfect control.

He launched as a topic of conversation the modern young person, and at just that moment I was grateful to him, although it is a subject which, as far as I am concerned, has been thoroughly talked out. Ordinarily I find myself desperately bored with the solemn and terrified generalities one hears. I like the young people of today, but as for the modern young person, considered as something essentially new, a product of post-war conditions or a judgment upon our sins, I simply don't believe the little monster exists.

I didn't, however, express myself in this destructive manner to Mr. Smith. I coddled the topic along. Anything was welcome that would keep us away from the tangled skein of fact that Judy seemed involved in.

"Manners change, I admit," I said, "but manners are by definition conventional conduct, conduct which has no significance one way or the other. Think of this wedding. Judy's going to be married in the garden, and her bridesmaids, from what I hear of the costumes, are going to look more or less like a chorus in a light opera. It will be an amazingly pretty picture, no doubt. But Victoria in her day would as soon have thought of being married in a bathing suit. Victoria would have been horrified at the idea of sleeping the night before her wedding under the same roof with the man she was going to marry. Victoria was supposed to be shy, so she acted as if she were. But that doesn't mean that she was any finer or cleaner-minded than Judy is. No, the younger generation...."

My argument was interrupted.

"Here comes a sample of it now," said Mr. Smith, who was gazing down the path. "Heavens, that's not Punch, is it?"

It was though, and he was a good sight; hatless as always, and clad in khaki shirt and trousers which went well with his brown skin. He was carrying his little target rifle.

There was no doubt that he was coming to make me a visit, for he waved gaily toward the summer-house as he came along. He and I both got a surprise, though, out of his meeting with Mr. Smith; Punch because he hadn't had the least idea he'd find him with me, and I over the discovery that they were old friends. They greeted each other with enthusiasm.

"I hadn't realized you were so well acquainted," said I.

"Oh, yes," Punch told me; "we're very old friends. Mr. Smith was the nicest man in Paris that winter we lived there. He used to take me around and show me things.

"My, but I'm glad you're here," he went on, turning back to the old gentleman. "It comes out just right. But why aren't you over at our house?"

"Your mother asked me to take him in," I explained. "She thought you'd be too wild for him over there; too much row, late hours and so on."

"Ho!" said Punch derisively to his very old friend, "there couldn't be too much row for you, could there?"

I thought I saw a troubled look coming into the boy's eyes, so I changed the subject.

"You out shooting rabbits?" I asked.

"No," he said. "I haven't shot anything yet."

"After bigger game perhaps," Mr. Smith suggested. "Lions, or hippo-potamuses."

"No," said Punch, "I'm not hunting *anything*, really."

"You aren't *being* hunted, are you?" Mr. Smith wanted to know.

I thought the boy flushed a little.

"No, I guess not," he said.

"I suppose," the old man suggested, "if they're keeping such late hours over at The Oaks, the mornings must be pretty slow."

"Yes," Punch admitted, "they are, rather. Oh, everybody's up but no-body's doing anything. Nobody but Bruce Applebury. He went off to town on the morning train, with Judy."

I don't know what happened to my face at that, but I can answer for Mr. Smith's. There wasn't a flicker of an eyelid to betray anything.

Punch was looking at him just as I was, and he went on, "He's the man who's going to marry Judy, you know. He was afraid he wouldn't get the sort of wedding ring she liked, so he took her in today to pick it out." He sighed and added, "I'll be glad when this business is all over."

"How's your grandmother?" Mr. Smith asked.

"Oh, she's better this morning, now that she knows the necklace has come back," the boy said. "Of course it was an awful shock to her last night when she found it had been stolen."

I'd been holding my breath waiting for this to happen, from the moment I had seen how friendly was the relation between the old gentleman and the boy, but I hadn't expected it to come out with a plop like that. I felt rather embarrassed over my own reticence, but Mr. Smith didn't even indirectly reproach me with it.

"I didn't know the necklace had been stolen," he said. "I've only just got here, you see. Tell me about it."

"There's Donovan," I pointed out. "He's coming up to tell us lunch is ready, I expect. You'll stay, won't you, Punch? And then you can tell Mr. Smith the whole story of how the necklace was stolen. And perhaps," I added, "you'll tell me, too, the details of how it came back."

For I didn't see any point, now that the cat had got out, in trying to make a mystery of the empty bag.

I was relieved, though, that Punch's story, which he told with admirable lucidity at lunch time, was considerably abridged where it touched Judy. Of course at that time I knew nothing of the letter that had been pushed through the narrow neck of the Chinese vase, nor of her nocturnal excursion for its recovery. Punch's account of his adventures that night left this episode out.

He told us how, when he couldn't sleep in his room on the top floor, he'd come down to the davenport in the hall below; how he'd seen a man in pajamas going up-stairs; how the mystery had completely baffled him at the time; how Miss Digby had told him of the fright she'd had, and how, between sleep and waking he'd figured out what had happened.

"Good work, Punch," Mr. Smith said, when the tale was told. "I'm proud of you." His tone, though, wasn't as enthusiastic as his words. He'd spoken with only half his mind, as if out of some deep preoccupation.

"Well, that's more than anybody else is," the boy answered. "You see they all think—mother and Miss Digby and Uncle Alec—that I took the necklace myself, for a joke or something, and then brought it back in the middle of the night. It's what anybody would think if they didn't believe the story of the man in the pajamas. And it *is* sort of a funny story. Only, you see, I *saw* him."

"Yes," Mr. Smith said thoughtfully, "it is a funny story, sure enough."

The boy looked from one of us to the other, possibly to satisfy himself that we ourselves believed it. He must have done so, for presently he went on.

"It gets even funnier than that. Because, you see, as long as they thought I'd done it, I wanted to know whose pajamas I'd seen, and who it probably was who wore them. So after they'd all gone down to breakfast, I went around and saw all the pajamas there were—all that had been slept in, I mean—and I couldn't find the pair I'd seen last night. They weren't on the top floor, so I went down to the second floor, and they weren't there either."

"Are you sure you saw them all?" Mr. Smith asked.

"I counted," said Punch. "I found a pair for everybody."

"Servants too?" Mr. Smith asked.

"No," said Punch. "But you see there isn't any third floor to the servants' wing. The door to it opens into the second-floor hall where the davenport is. If it had been one of the servants he wouldn't have gone up-stairs."

"How well did you see the pajamas when the man was wearing them?" I asked.

"Pretty well," Punch said. "I saw the legs of them awfully well, because they walked right through the moonlight and it was about as bright as day. They were plain pajamas, gray, or some color like that, and one of the legs was torn, a little square tear as if it had been caught on a nail. Well, the only person in the house whose pajamas are plain gray is Uncle Alec, and they weren't torn. Besides he's about twice as big as the man I saw. Everybody else's pajamas are fancy; because of the wedding, I suppose. Anyhow, it's a puzzle."

"Well, the pearls are brought back, that's one thing," Mr. Smith observed. "To your grandmother's room, you say? Where are they now?"

Punch's eye gleamed with a sudden pleasure. "That's supposed to be a great secret," he said.

"Don't tell any secrets," Mr. Smith warned him quickly.

"Well, it isn't a secret from you—from either of you," Punch explained. "And Donovan isn't around, is he, nor anyone else who'd hear?"

"No," I said, "you won't be overheard. But how do you know we're not to be kept out of the secret?"

"I'll tell you," he said, "and then you'll see. It's a secret from mother, all right, and Judy and Uncle Alec, but not from you.

"It was when I was going around on the second floor, looking at the pajamas, that grandmother heard me and called me into her room. She said I'd been right about the safe not being a safe place for the necklace, so she was going to give it to me to hide. Only I was to promise not to tell anyone in the house that she'd done it, nor where the necklace was, of course. But you see, you aren't in the house, so the secret doesn't include you."

I won't pretend to have been satisfied that this bit of casuistry was strong enough to bear, but my curiosity was much wider awake, just then, than my conscience. I made no protest, and neither did Mr. Smith. The boy went on:

"Mother came in just after Gran had given it to me and asked her where it was, and Gran told her it was in the safe. She'd had me put the box back in the safe and lock the safe up, but of course the box was empty. Mother asked her when she was going to give the necklace to Judy, and Gran said she would when she got ready. She always gets kind of cross when you ask her a lot of questions. So mother saw it was no good asking more and went away. And there I had it all the time."

"Where did you hide it?" Mr. Smith asked.

Punch was thoroughly enjoying himself now, there could be no doubt of that. The unjust accusations of his mother and Uncle Alec and old Digs he could afford to ignore in the face of this magnificent compensation.

"Why, I thought of lots of places," he said, "that would probably have been all right, but I didn't like them somehow, and then I thought about *The Purloined Letter*—you know, that story of Poe's. How the safest hiding-place for anything is the last place where anyone would think of looking for it. So I just wrapped the necklace up in a handkerchief and stuck it in my pocket."

"Good lord!" I cried. "Is that where it is now?"

"Surely it is," old Mr. Smith remarked calmly. "Hence the rifle."

Punch flushed a little. "Of course it's only a twenty-two," he said, "but it's got a long cartridge in it."

At first blush the idea of entrusting a famous jewel like the Corbin necklace to the trousers pocket of a thirteen-year-old boy armed with a little target rifle seemed wild enough, and when one added that an inexplicable attempt had just been made to steal it, an attempt that might be repeated at any hour, day or night, it became perfectly frantic. I didn't care much about the necklace, but I cared immensely about the boy.

He was looking eagerly into my face, and must have read the consternation that was printed plain upon it. "Can you think of a safer place?" he asked. "Of course I suppose I could give it to you to keep for me."

"Heaven forbid!" I cried. "But there must be some other...."

I let the sentence fade out unfinished, and lapsed into a thoughtful silence. I couldn't think of anything better, and that was the truth.

"It's years since I've seen that string of pearls," Mr. Smith said presently. "Let's have a look at them, Punch."

The boy plunged a hand deep into his pocket and pulled out a wadded and rather grimy handkerchief which he spread open on the table. There the thing was, all right. I stared at it fascinated.

It was beautiful, of course, that perfectly graded series of shining globes, but I was moved by the sight of it to reflect how ridiculously artificial our values are. That thing would buy leisure for a man's lifetime. Comparatively few men from the cradle to the grave are able by their labors to earn as much as would be needed to buy it. Numberless men alive in the world today would commit any crime up to murder to possess it. It seemed absurd when one thought of it like that.

Possibly to carry out the illusion the thing wanted a better background. Perhaps it suffered from the indignity of contact with a small boy's pocket handkerchief.

Old Mr. Smith took the thing in his fingers—unusually intelligent-looking old fingers they were, as if habituated to handling pearls. Then I glanced up at his face, and was struck by a conviction which for the moment put the necklace clean out of my mind.

He had stuck a monocle into one eye. The gleam may have come merely from the lens, but from wherever it came, there was so piercing a brilliancy in his gaze that I almost shouted, "Old Eagle-Eye!" aloud.

I didn't, of course. He went on studying the necklace, and Punch sat gazing from his face to mine. Of course—of course! Why hadn't I identified him at once? He was the man Judy was to prevent, at all costs, from getting a chance at something—the necklace, beyond a doubt. That was why Victoria hadn't wanted to keep him in the house.

Well, the best laid plans go wrong sometimes. Victoria had overdone it. There sat old Eagle-Eye with the necklace in his hands.

What was he going to do with it? I'll admit that in my confounded state of mind I'd hardly have been surprised at anything. I didn't really expect him to perpetrate a robbery with violence then and there, but I was vividly conscious, for a fleeting instant, that Punch's little rifle was leaning up in the corner of the room, far out of reach. It only shows what an atmosphere of persistent mystery will do to the ordinarily well-behaved mind.

Mr. Smith, however, remained calm, and when he had done examining the necklace, folded it up again in Punch's handkerchief, rather negligently I thought, and handed it over to the boy.

"Put it back in your pocket, Punch," he said. "I can't think of a safer place for it. But now that you've gratified our curiosity," he went on, "I think you'd better stretch the promise you gave your grandmother to include everybody, out of the house as well as in it. Who are in the house, anyway? Do you know them all?"

"Oh, hardly any of them, if you mean do I *really* know, not just who they're supposed to be. I don't think mother does, even; not the Applebury crowd."

"And the Appleburys," commented Mr. Smith, "don't know Judy's crowd any better. It's a perfect situation, in a way."

We weren't very talkative during the rest of the lunch. The thoughts of old Eagle-Eye seemed to be running mostly on the man in pajamas.

"You said he wasn't near as big as your Uncle Alec. Was he noticeably small; smaller, say, than any of the men in the party?"

"No," Punch said, "I don't think he was. He just looked about ordinary. Of course, I didn't see him very well, except his legs, and I didn't look at him very hard. I just thought he was somebody going to the bathroom, until he started up-stairs. I think he looked sort of stout and clumsy, as if he filled his pajamas rather full."

"Are you sure it *was* a man. I know you didn't think of it at the time, but mayn't it have been a woman? I believe they wear pajamas sometimes. And in any sort of men's clothes they're likely to look heavy."

I could see that the idea attracted Punch. It seemed to offer a loophole of escape from his mystery. But he was too honest a witness to avail himself of it.

"No," he said, "I don't think it was. I don't think a woman would have walked along like that."

"You're probably right," the old man agreed. "Most women would look like women even if they had on a man's pajamas. We'll stick to the men for the present. Stout and stocky, medium height; does that describe anybody in the party?"

Punch laughed. "The only one it describes is Bruce Applebury himself," he said.

Mr. Smith didn't laugh. "What are *his* pajamas like?" he asked.

"Sort of tan color," said Punch, "with red stripes."

I spoke up in the interests of common sense. "Surely you couldn't suspect...."

"I'd suspect anybody," the old man asserted, "when we're concerned with a thing like that necklace. Oh, not suspect if you dislike the word—but consider as possibly involved. I admit my point of view is rather specialized."

"He played tennis and swam practically from the time he came to the house until he dressed for dinner," I pointed out, "and the loss of the necklace was discovered before he'd finished dressing."

"Probably, then, he didn't take it," Mr. Smith conceded. "But he may have brought it back, and that's just as important a part of the mystery."

Without waiting to allow time for that to sink in, he turned to Punch. "When is he—when are he and Judy expected back from town?" he asked.

"There's a train about three. I think they'll surely come on that, because they're going to rehearse the wedding this afternoon. You'll come over for that, won't you?"

Eagle-Eye took this invitation with a twinkle. "Old men are supposed to take naps after lunch," he said. "Still, I may turn up. If I do, suppose, since we're already in mystery up to the neck, that you greet me as if we were meeting for the first time since Paris. Can we get away with it? Did anybody know you were coming here to lunch?"

"No," said Punch. "I just sort of disappeared. I suppose I'd better be going back now, though, or they may begin wondering where I am. I *could* eat another lunch, of course."

We both laughed over that as we bade him farewell. But we turned pretty serious as we watched him walk away with his little rifle.

"Do you think he's safe going around with a hundred-thousand-dollar necklace in his pocket?" I asked.

"Yes, I think so," Mr. Smith answered reflectively. "For one thing, he hasn't got it in his pocket."

I must have gaped at him like a goggle-eyed fish. My mind once more had gone to pieces. Had the old gentleman done a sleight of hand trick when he returned that handkerchief?

"Oh, he's got just what he brought over here with him," he added. "Undoubtedly the same thing his grandmother gave him this morning to hide for her. It's not the necklace. It's a very fair imitation of it, however."

"You're perfectly sure of that, I suppose?" I asked weakly.

He nodded.

"You'd better go back to your couch where you'll be comfortable," he suggested. "We've got some thinking to do."

I agreed, and rang for Donovan. When he'd made me comfortable and gone away, Mr. Smith pulled up an easy chair for himself and lighted a cigar.

"I know that necklace intimately," he began. "I sold it to Punch's grandfather in Paris, 'way back in the days of the Second Empire. Lord, what a while ago! A man shouldn't be allowed to live as long as that. Eighteen hundred seventy it must have been, or thereabouts.

"I'm a jeweler by profession, and I was managing director over there for Paulding and Revere. I've seen the necklace a number of times since. Mrs. Corbin always gave me a look at it whenever she came to Paris. So I can say with certainty that the thing Punch has in his pocket is not merely a necklace of imitation pearls; it's an imitation, pearl for pearl, of that necklace. In fact, we can go a little further than that, if you don't mind my prosing a bit."

"I don't," I assured him.

"Both the French and the Japanese make imitation pearls," he went on. "Serious imitations, I mean. Merely for purposes of wear, the French pearls are better. Their luster's more like the real thing. On a pretty woman's neck in a ballroom they wouldn't be detected as not the real thing. But the moment you pick them up, they give themselves away. They're much too light and much too translucent. Japanese pearls, on the other hand, are the right weight, or very near it, and they don't betray themselves when you hold them against the light. But they haven't the luster, not even the best of them.

"Well, these are Japanese pearls. Whoever had the string made of them, it's fair to assume, wanted them for some other purpose than wearing to parties. The French pearls would have been better for that, and cheaper too. But they wouldn't serve if they had to deceive someone who had opportunities to handle them."

"In other words they were made to deceive old Mrs. Corbin," I broke in. "Her eyesight has been failing for years."

"That's very likely a good guess," he said mildly. "But let's not begin guessing just yet.

"She may have ordered the imitation made herself. She's as likely to have wanted to deceive Victoria, let us say, as Victoria is to have wanted to deceive her. And with her poor vision she may have deceived herself. The real string may have been knocking about, unregarded for months, in some drawer of her dressing-table, while the imitation was lying in the safe.

"All we know is that there are two strings, and that a person who couldn't see very well, either because his eyes were bad, or because he was working in the dark, might easily mistake one for the other. We know that the imitation string is now in Punch's pocket. But where the real string is we don't know."

"It's reasonably probable, isn't it," I asked, "that the necklace in Punch's pocket is the same one that his grandmother showed him Wednesday afternoon, when she told him she meant to give it to Judy for a wedding present? It was taken from the safe, it was brought back, and it was handed by his grandmother straight to Punch."

"That's as good a possibility as any," said the old man. "The thief takes it in a hurry and more or less in the dark, discovers at his first good look at it that it's an imitation, and brings it back. But there are other hypotheses just as good.

"He may have seen a chance to take the real one at a time when he hadn't the imitation at hand to replace it with, and then brought the imitation back in the hope that the loss hadn't yet been discovered. It wasn't made public, I understand. Or someone may have borrowed the real one and returned the imitation by mistake. Or one person may have stolen the real one, and someone else, who later discovered the theft and wished to shield the thief, may have brought back the imitation, thinking he was making restitution. You see, it's endless. The most serious mistake we can make will be to begin thinking we know too much."

"Of course," I agreed. "One could easily do a cruel injustice to an innocent person by jumping at conclusions."

"That's not just what I mean," he said gently. "Perhaps I should have said dangerous instead of serious. I'm more concerned over what may happen in the next twenty-four hours than I am over what may have happened—oh, any time within the last five years."

He gave me half a moment of silence to digest that in.

"I'll run the risk of speaking with the utmost plainness," he then went on. "I think I can guess how this thing looks to you. You believe Victoria had that imitation string made for the purpose of imposing upon her mother-in-law and getting possession of the real one. You think she took alarm over Mrs. Corbin's decision to give it to Judy, because she thought that such a gift would lead to the discovery of the substitution and that she'd be charged with it. You think that's why she didn't want me stopping in the house.

"That's all plausible enough. It may all be true. It would account, after a fashion, for the disappearance of the imitation necklace from the safe. She might have taken it herself; she might have persuaded Judy to take it.

"But into that picture you can not fit the return of the necklace. You can't fit the man in pajamas, whom Punch saw. I have no intelligible picture, yet, into which that man will fit. But the return, I tell you frankly, seems to me to be sinister. It suggests strongly the presence somewhere, as an active possibility, of the real necklace—not stolen yet, but waiting to be. And accompanying that theft we may have anything, up to murder. That's why I say it's dangerous to feel too sure."

With great deliberation, he extinguished his cigar in the ash tray and rose to his full height.

"Invited or not," he said, "I'm going to that house this afternoon. I want to see the people in it. There aren't a great many first-class jewel thieves in the world, and I know the faces of a pretty fair proportion of them. Of course people who aren't jewel thieves sometimes attempt to steal jewels—a covetous girl, a boy desperately in debt, might make a frantic clutch, with no forethought, no preparation, and of course, no possibility of ultimate success.

"If that's the case here, I'm as helpless as any of you, for I can't read thoughts or intentions from people's faces.

"But somehow to me the thing hasn't quite that look. So I'm going over to see whether I know any of Victoria's guests better than she does. How about you? Will you come along? Can you manage in a comfortable motor, if you've lots of room?"

I could manage it, all right, and my first impulse was to say I'd go. Then I thought of something and changed my mind.

"I think I'll stay at home this afternoon," I told him, "and rest up for that dinner."

CHAPTER IX

MYSTIFICATION OF EAGLE-EYE

It was the thought of Judy that made me change my mind about going to The Oaks with old Mr. Smith. I thought that perhaps if I were alone at the cottage all afternoon, and if the fact that I was here alone were advertised by the presence of my ancient guest at The Oaks, she might come back and tell me the story which he had prevented my hearing at the summer-house.

My concern for the child was fast deepening into an acute distress. I was spared, to be sure, the misery of doubting her essential rectitude. I'd known her from the time she was a baby, and the long intervals when I'd seen nothing of her had neither interrupted the growth of our friendship, nor changed the quality of it.

She'd never been expansively confidential; reticence was, indeed, one of her outstanding qualities. Victoria complained of her as a close-mouthed little thing who kept everything to herself. But candor—perhaps I shouldn't put it that way, for I believe the two things naturally go together—candor was not a virtue with her, but simply an irresistible compulsion. She couldn't even acquiesce at all graciously in a pretense. I consider myself a decently straightforward person, but I've been self-convicted a dozen times by a straight look from Judy's eyes of cowardly flinchings from the plain truth. I don't think she regards them as cowardly. She isn't a bit of a prig. She simply doesn't understand how it can be done.

The pungent quality of cynicism which sometimes flavors her speech has always one source—sham. She is cynical of shams.

I recalled a remark she had made to me only a day or two before, to the effect that the horridest thing in the world was whitewash. Then, with a start, I remembered the prediction she'd made in the next breath that she was going to be coated with it this week. How much had she known about the necklace then? Anything more than was involved in the newspaper announcement that her grandmother was going to give it to her as a wedding present?

In the light of Mr. Smith's revelations this afternoon, I thought it likely that she had known more; known that the necklace then reposing in the Morocco-covered box in her grandmother's safe was an imitation, and that the fact somehow involved her mother's credit. Didn't an invincible determination on Judy's part to save her mother's credit account for everything the girl was doing—including, even, her agreement to marry a man whom she didn't love?

It was all very well for old Mr. Smith, whose emotions were running cool and thin, to warn me against jumping at conclusions. But I had to jump. I had nowhere else to go. So I nailed my conviction like a flag to this mast.

It wasn't necessary to try to work out all the details. Victoria had done something—probably, in some desperate money crisis, stolen the necklace; she'd always believed it was going to be hers some day—and Judy had agreed to see her through.

How had that involved a marriage with Bruce Applebury? Possibly Victoria had sold the necklace to him. Or possibly she'd done something besides steal the necklace. (I found it comparatively easy, that afternoon, to impute anything to Victoria.) At all events the necklace, the real one, had to be recovered, somehow.

Was this the errand Judy and Bruce had started upon, this morning under the innocent pretense of buying the wedding ring? Had she really started with him and been compelled, by some unforeseen occurrence, to turn back? Or had she only pretended to go with him in order to be free for some other meeting, under the protection of his cousin?

What sort of rendezvous had my unexpected visit to the summer-house prevented? Had old Mr. Smith, through my field-glasses, caught a glimpse of the other party to it?

I had an exciting feeling, about then, that I was within one idea of the solution. But this idea, widely as I cast my net for it, refused to be caught. And presently my little pattern, fragmentary as it was, fell to pieces again.

How was I going to account for the theft of the imitation necklace and for the return of it? Well, I didn't care about that. That didn't necessarily concern Judy at all.

But how about the thing that had happened to her on the veranda yesterday afternoon when the guests were arriving? The thing that had set her world rocking like a boat, that had led her to cry out to Punch, "Are you on my side, whatever happens—whatever I do?" No, I couldn't solve that. I wanted her to come and tell me about it. She didn't come, though, and I put in the longest, dreariest afternoon I can remember, waiting for her.

When Mr. Ethelbert Smith returned about six o'clock I was in so detestably unamiable a state of mind that a resolute summoning of all the manners I had ever learned hardly availed to produce a decent show of politeness. I didn't want, I told myself, any more of his cold-hearted observations. However, common civility required me to ask for them, and before he had gone very far I was listening with unfeigned interest.

He began with an apology. He had permitted himself this morning to be saddled upon me as a guest, and now, after I'd hospitably made him welcome, and most comfortable, he added, he was about to climb out of the saddle again. In short, he was about to pack his bags and go to The Oaks to stay.

It appeared that old Mrs. Corbin, who'd been, of course, the first person he'd asked for on arriving at the house, had seen him at once and made him welcome in the friendliest manner. Furthermore she'd been furiously annoyed to learn that he was not stopping under her roof, and had insisted that he change his plans at once in order to do so.

"She's altered greatly—by illness, of course," he remarked, "but she's no less imperious than she was in her best days. She settled the matter of my entertainment then and there, and summoned Victoria as tyrannically as she would have sent for her chambermaid. Victoria came, too."

"Was she startled at finding you there?" I asked.

"If she was, she didn't show it. She may have been warned, of course; probably was. A question or two of the servant who brought the message would have let her know what she had to expect. No, she took my being there as the most natural thing in the world. She didn't show more than a flicker or two of resentment over the manner in which the orders were given. She must, of course, be in a state of suppressed rebellion all the time, for I fancy that sort of thing is an every-day occurrence. I'm sorry for Victoria. I wouldn't blame her much for anything she might resort to, short of poison, as an escape."

"Did you find out anything about the necklace?" I asked. "From the old lady herself, I mean? Whether she knows of the existence of the imitation one?"

"I was disappointed there," Mr. Smith said. "I thought that when Victoria had gone, Mrs. Corbin would unburden her mind. She has something weighing upon it, I should say. But the emotion she'd wasted over the matter of where I was to sleep had completely exhausted her. She had to ring for her nurse, and tell me we'd have our visit later. She wasn't visible again all the afternoon. So I was told, at least, and of course I couldn't question it."

Then, "Do you know anything about that nurse?" he asked.

"She's been with Mrs. Corbin two or three years," I told him. "Punch regards her humorously, I think, but considers her above suspicion. Why? Did you notice anything queer about her?"

"When I left Mrs. Corbin's room," he said, "she was parting from Victoria in the hall. Evidently they'd been talking somewhere. It struck me that the woman was frightfully upset—frightened or shocked, I couldn't tell which. She might have been found out in something, or she might have been given some order she didn't want to carry out. They aren't drugging that old lady, are they?"

"She drugs herself, I understand—morphine. Naturally enough, after years of pain."

He looked like a very old man when I told him that, and he sat musing over it for a long time. Finally he roused himself.

"Well, I didn't find what I went for," he said. "I made a point of strolling about the house. I managed to see several of the servants; not all of them, of course. But in a talk I had with Punch, I asked him whether any new house servants had been taken on during the last two weeks, and he said there had not. Somehow I don't believe it's the servants we have to reckon with anyhow.

"I saw all the guests in the house eventually. There was quite a wait for the principal performers. The others were all gathered for the rehearsal of the ceremony, impatient as school children for it to be over with, too, so that they could run away and play. But Judy and the bridegroom, by failing for a long time to put in an appearance, kept them waiting."

"Was Bill Grant there?" I asked.

"He was. And his manner toward me excited my admiration. His weakness is evidently that he mustn't be surprised. Do you remember him this morning, completely disconcerted, unable to contribute more than a disjointed word here and there to the talk, floundering in the presence of the unexpected? But evidently he'd foreseen the probability of an encounter with me this afternoon, and he sustained it with complete *sang froid*. Everybody else was discussing Judy's trip to town with her bridegroom. Nobody questioned but that was where she was spending the day. He knew that I knew that she hadn't gone to town, that she'd spent the day, or a good part of it, surreptitiously with him. Yet he confronted me without batting an eye, without attempting a private explanation, or even a private signal entreating me not to give them away. He was, I felt, in the circumstances almost formidably self-possessed.

"His self-possession didn't last him through the afternoon, however. Fate had another surprise in store for him."

"What was the surprise?" I asked.

"That's the point of my story," he said. "But let me tell it in order. The fact that it doesn't make sense makes it more important to approach it methodically.

"Before Judy arrived with her bridegroom, I had seen every one of the guests in that house, including Mr. Alexander Corbin and excepting only the bridegroom himself. There was no one among them whom I recognized as a professional jewel thief. Mr. Bruce Applebury then arrived with Judy and I didn't recognize him either. I had drawn blank as far as my particular errand to the house was concerned. But I was diverted from thoughts of my failure by something I saw happening under my eyes.

"I saw enacted a scene of perfectly tragic intensity, and I haven't the remotest idea now what it meant. I can tell it all in a very few words, because the scene itself had no accompanying words at all.

"Judy, as I say, arrived in the car with Mr. Bruce Applebury. They were surrounded at once by a group of young people who had been waiting for them on the lawn, clamoring for the rehearsal to begin. I looked at Mr. Applebury, realized that I didn't know him and realized, further, that I didn't like him. He is self-important and oppressively correct. He looked not sulky, exactly—mulish, that's better. And victorious. Like a bad-tempered parent who has just beaten one of his children and has succeeded in persuading himself of his own righteousness.

"As for Judy, she was like an automaton; an amazingly life-like, well-made automaton, capable of going where she should, answering questions, even of responding in an appropriate manner to jokes. Perhaps I shouldn't have perceived how perfectly galvanic all this was if I hadn't happened to be standing where I intercepted the one look she turned upon her mother.

"It was a look—it's a strong word, but I mean it—of horror, the look of one still incredulous over a betrayal. Something had happened to her that had never entered into her calculations as a possibility when we saw her in the summer-house this morning, although I thought she was facing some rather queer possibilities then."

I couldn't bear to have it spun out any longer. "What happened?" I demanded. "Get to the point, man, and tell me."

"Nothing happened," he said. "Nothing, at least, until after the scene was over. They went ahead and had their rehearsal. I watched. I watched all of them, even Alexander Corbin. Particularly I watched our young friend Bill Grant.

"He had already had his surprise. But I swear I don't know how he got it. He hadn't had a significant look or word, let alone an intelligible message, either from his cousin or from Judy. And yet he looked like a man in a daze. When it came time for him to produce the ring and hand it to the bridegroom, a good stiff nudge was not enough to bring him to. He had to be spoken to, and then he responded like a somnambulist.

"I simply can't describe the intensity of the feeling that was shared, in some inexplicable way, by Judy and those two young men. And what made a nightmare of it was that no one seemed to perceive it but myself. Oh, Victoria may have been a little unnaturally alert. She'd taken that look from Judy square in the face; though without flinching, so that I wonder now whether she knew what it meant. To the others it was simply the rehearsal of a wedding, to the usual accompaniment of jokes and giggles."

"How about Punch? Didn't he see anything?"

"No, I don't think he did. He was entirely serious, of course; scrupulous about doing his part exactly as he was told. One of his hands showed a tendency to stray into his pocket, but he corrected that when his mother spoke to him about it. No, Punch had something else on his mind and I don't think he saw a thing.

"Yet I can swear that if those three people had been Italians, there'd have been a flash of a stiletto. But who would have wielded it and who'd have got it, I don't know.

"Something did happen at last, just when the rehearsal was over. Someone, perhaps two or three of them at once, said to Applebury, 'Now's when you kiss her.'

"Judy turned to him and said, without any expression in her face at all, 'Are you going to? You can if you like, of course.'

"He went rather red and stood looking at her like a fool. Angry I should say, rather than embarrassed. I don't think he'd embarrass easily. He has no misgivings about himself.

"She didn't give him more than a second to make up his mind. Then she reached out a hand for the other man. Some fool laughed and said, 'Are you going to kiss him instead?', but nobody else made that mistake. Something about her gesture silenced the lot of them.

"She said right out so that everybody could hear, 'I'm going to talk to Bill for five minutes, over on that bench.' She nodded toward a stone seat at the bottom of the lawn in plain sight, but out of earshot. 'After that we'll decide what we're going to do next.' She led young Grant off to the bench and they sat down on it with their backs to us.

"There was some electricity in the air by then. I think that for a moment Applebury considered following her, but he changed his mind about it, and turned to Victoria. The others stayed together in a group, as if they didn't know what to do nor where to look.

"I looked frankly at the pair on the bench. They sat side by side, not very close together though, and talked without looking at each other. It didn't last very long; less, I'm sure, than the five minutes Judy stipulated. Then she got up, turned away from him, still without a look, and came back toward us, he following.

"She looked to me then a perfectly live girl. The second act of *The Tales of Hoffman* was over. 'It's too late and too hot for tennis,' she said. 'Let's all go for a swim in the pool.'

"I heard Grant speak to her just before they got within the hearing of the others. 'I'll think of something, yet,' he said. She answered him over her shoulder for anybody to hear that might. 'All right, if you can.' He'd got over his surprise at all events and seemed to be coming to life again, himself.

"He went into the pool with the others. So did Judy. So did everybody except Punch and Bruce Applebury. One of the bridesmaids made quite a point of it that Punch should go in; a personal appeal. But he refused regretfully, and I knew why. His bathing suit hadn't any pocket in it.

"I don't know why Applebury didn't go in. He looked hot and stuffy enough after his day in town. Unless..."

Old Eagle-Eye's face suddenly brightened and he slapped his lean old leg. "Unless, by George, he had the same reason that Punch had, only a better one. Do you suppose he had the real necklace in his pocket?"

"Damn the necklace!" I cried.

"Damn it by all means," he agreed seriously. "But in the meantime we'd better be dressing for dinner. You're going, aren't you?"

I told him dully that I didn't think I would.

But after he'd gone up-stairs to change his clothes and pack, a servant from The Oaks brought me a note from Judy that changed my mind.

"You must come tonight," it said. "Not that you can do anything, but I want you here."

CHAPTER X

TRANSFORMATION SCENE

What Judy thought she wanted of me at dinner that night I don't know. Probably she didn't know herself. She regarded me as an ally and may have reasoned that some unforeseen change in the pattern of things might make me useful. Or, more likely, she didn't reason at all; just felt that she wanted me there, and sent for me.

As things turned out, the part I played at the dinner was merely that of a wholly unimportant spectator. The cue that called me upon the stage wasn't given me until several hours later. Neither during the dinner nor after it did I have a moment alone with her.

I had a little talk with Punch, though, and got one curious piece of information from him. That this happened was due to our somewhat too prompt arrival at The Oaks. Belden had taken old Mr. Smith up-stairs to show him his room, and the boy, who was the first one of The Oaks party to appear in the drawing-room, seated himself on the arm of the easy chair where the butler had deposited me, and brought his report down to date.

"Have you still got it?" I asked.

He patted his trousers pocket confidentially.

"I didn't forget to change it when I changed my clothes," he told me, "and I bolted my door and hung my coat on the door-knob. So nobody knows where it is. Mother thinks it's still in the safe. I don't know what I'll do about it tonight, though, after I've gone to bed. Sleep with my trousers on, I expect. Unless grandmother has me give it back to her before then."

"Have you any idea that she means to?" I asked.

"Well," he said, "of course you never can tell about Gran. She called me into her room again just now and asked me if it was safe, and if I had it hidden where I could get it when it was wanted. I said I could. She's coming down to dinner tonight, you know, and she may spring something. I'll be all ready if she does."

He grinned and added, "It certainly will be a surprise for mother."

"How do you know she thinks it's in the safe?" I asked.

He hesitated, and I didn't know for a minute whether he meant to answer. His pride over what he felt to be a sound piece of reasoning, and his wish to see whether or not I would follow it prevailed over any other feelings he may have had.

"It's kind of funny," he said. "I figured it out from Digs. You see, early this morning when I showed her that the necklace was back, she was awfully excited and said she thought I'd taken it for a joke—because I hated her, she said. She didn't mean that really—it was just because she was upset—and she came around later and said she was sorry. So that was all right.

"But this afternoon just before they had the wedding rehearsal Digs was all stirred up again. I saw she was acting sort of reproachful toward me, so I asked her what the matter was, and she said she didn't think it was fair of me to have told mother about her knowing the combination to the safe. She said she wasn't supposed to know it, only she had to in order to tell grandmother what it was when she forgot.

"Well, of course, I hadn't told mother that Digs knew the combination. I hadn't told anybody but you and Mr. Smith. And I told Digs I hadn't told mother. And then, because it seemed kind of funny, I asked Digs what made her think I had.

"She pressed her lips together—you know the sort of face she makes—and wasn't going to tell me.

"I said, 'Mother hasn't been accusing you of taking the necklace, has she?'

"She was very indignant then, and said, 'No, she has not,' and then she began to cry, and asked me if I'd miss her if she went away; because, she said, she thought she might have to.

"I asked her why, and she wouldn't tell me. So I said she mustn't mind grandmother even if she did get sort of rough sometimes, and Digs said she didn't mind grandmother. It wasn't that at all. She wouldn't say anything more; wanted to kiss me instead. So I went away to think about it."

I remembered old Mr. Smith's comment on Miss Digby's manner just after she'd parted from Victoria in the hall that afternoon. "Frightened—or shocked," he had said, and he had hazarded a guess that she might have been given some order that she didn't want to carry out. I didn't mention this to the boy, however. I waited to see what conclusion he'd come to by himself.

"I think," he went on, "that mother must have asked Digs to open the safe for her; just guessed that she might know the combination. And the only thing she'd want the safe open for would be to get the necklace out. I don't know why she wants to get it out, though, unless to put it in some safer place. Or unless"—he hung fire a moment but he couldn't turn aside from the pursuit of truth wherever it took him—"or unless mother doesn't think Gran ought to give Judy the necklace and wants to put it for a while somewhere so that she can't. Anyhow, it makes it sort of exciting about tonight, doesn't it?"

I cordially agreed that it did.

I don't think Victoria really expected me to come to the dinner, but with a crowd like that—there were more than thirty of us—one more or less couldn't have mattered much. They solved the problem of my stiff leg by putting me at a card table and giving me a spare chair opposite for my foot. I had Punch on one side of me and his special bridesmaid on the other. Either she was an uncommonly nice girl, or else the cradle and the grave, so to speak, were her specialties, for apparently she didn't mind in the least having us for her partners. She was very jolly anyhow and deserved a less divided attention than I was able to give her.

The rest of the elderly group sat at a table by themselves; old Mr. Ethelbert Smith at Mrs. Corbin's right at the head of it, Alec at the foot, and Victoria half-way down the side that faced me. The bridal party, lacking the two who had been told off to me, sat, eighteen in all, at an enormous table transversely to the room, Judy at the end of it nearest me, with Bill Grant at her right and Bruce away down at the other end.

The arrangement had its importance for me—by that same token it was probably an unlucky one for the nice bridesmaid—since it put all of the principal actors in the drama, or at least all whom I took to be the principal actors, where I could watch their faces. Judy and old Mrs. Corbin I saw in profile; Bill Grant, Bruce Applebury and Victoria faced me squarely.

I didn't neglect the others. One by one I studied them intently. One of them, it seemed impossible to resist the conclusion, must have been Punch's man in pajamas, who, for some motive less explicable even than the one that had incited the taking of it, had returned the stolen necklace to old Mrs. Corbin's room last night. Would the same man walk again tonight, I wondered?

I think I know something of faces. They've been a serious part of my study, at all events, for many years. But there wasn't one within range of my vision which I could associate at all with an act like that.

Anyhow, that didn't comprise the whole story. That is to say, the theft and return of the necklace did not. Otherwise it would not have involved Judy. And there was no getting away from the fact that she was involved inextricably.

She was not now perhaps, as I looked at her, quite the lifeless mechanical thing, the talking doll, which old Eagle-Eye had described her to have been at the rehearsal of her wedding, but she was still a long way from any Judy I had ever known. She was laughing too much and talking too hard. They didn't converse decorously in pairs down at that table, but called to one another back and forth down the length of it, and oftenest of all I heard her voice, all aglitter, the lovely sensitive shades quite gone out of it. Yes, she was entangled in something.

But was it the necklace? The question asked itself so clearly and suddenly in my mind that I started at it. Had Judy a story of her own, which by pure coincidence had fallen thwartwise of the mystery of the necklace? Was the wordless drama old Eagle-Eye had seen enacted this afternoon between the girl and those two young men nothing but a plain tale of common human jealousy? Could the riddle be solved on that hypothesis?

"What *is* Judy doing back there?" the nice bridesmaid asked me. "You've been looking steadily past my shoulder without saying a word for about five minutes, and I'm too curious to be polite any longer."

"I'm afraid it's I who've been too curious to be polite," I apologized contritely. "And she isn't doing anything, really."

I was going on expatiating, rather feebly I'm afraid, on the feelings of an avowedly sentimental honorary uncle, when Mrs. Corbin cut me short by calling aloud in her vibrant, imperious old voice to Punch.

"Come here!" she commanded the boy. "I want to speak to you."

Everybody in the room seemed to realize that something was coming, for Punch walked to her side in complete silence and we all heard what she said to him.

"Go and get that thing I told you to keep for me. Get it and take it to Judy."

Her voice was harsh as she issued the order, and I saw her turn a sardonic look down the table at Victoria. But nobody paid any attention to that. They were all watching Punch, expecting, of course, that he'd turn and leave the room. Instead, he walked straight toward Judy. His grandmother's voice halted him.

"Go and get it first," she called.

"Oh, I have it here in my pocket," said Punch. And he pulled out, on the words, the same rather disgraceful handkerchief in which he'd exhibited the necklace to us at the lunch table.

I stopped watching him then, and turned my eyes, once more, on Judy. And, pearls or no pearls, she was the one to watch. The first look that flashed into her face when she saw what her brother was bringing her was one of an irrepressible disgust. She had damned the necklace, before, and this look of hers damned it now. That was gone, of course, in an instant, and by the time the others had turned to look at her, she had ironed out her face into a perfectly correct expression of pleasure over the receipt of a rather overwhelming gift—surprise and delight beautifully mingled.

She lifted the thing daintily from Punch's outrageous handkerchief, felt for the ends, and fastened it around her neck. I saw her fingers pause suddenly over the clasp, not so much as if they were baffled by it, but as if all the activities of her body had been, for an instant, frozen. Another instant and she had fastened the clasp, turned away from the table, and was coming down the length of the room toward her grandmother. She passed my chair on the way, but she had no eyes for me in that moment.

The girl's face was transfigured, her eyes were shining like stars. I can't help it if I am banal, it's what they were shining like. I heard her catch her breath in something like a sob as she walked by.

"Gran, you darling!" she cried. And rather to Mrs. Corbin's astonishment I think, she bent and kissed her squarely on her old mouth before the old woman had time to turn her cheek. "Are they *really* mine?" Judy demanded. "Do you mean you've *given* them to me?"

"They belong to you, and to no one else," Mrs. Corbin said. "Here! Give Ethelbert Smith a look at them. He knew them long before you were born, or your father, either."

The girl turned to him dutifully, leaning forward so that they swung away from her breast. I saw old Mr. Smith touch them with the tips of his fastidious fingers, and then I looked at Victoria.

She wasn't a beautiful sight. The change in color of her face had made the make-up blotchy, and her eyes were as hard as stones. I'm sure she wasn't breathing. But old Mr. Smith's voice came out suave and untroubled.

"The Corbin necklace is one of the most beautiful strings of pearls I know, my dear. And your young neck is worthy of it. I wish you happiness."

The other table broke up as Judy approached it. They all grouped around her to look and go into raptures. That was my first impression at least, but it was not quite correct.

Bruce Applebury expressed no raptures, and he fell back a little from the group, seeming content to survey this marvelous gift to his bride at long range. This might have been nothing, of course, but the celebrated Applebury reserve.

But there was none of that reserve about his cousin, Bill Grant. That young man didn't even pretend to look. And he was scowling just as he had scowled that morning when he and Judy had come upon me in the summer-house. But nobody, of course, was paying any attention to him.

Eventually the tumult subsided and people went back to their places. Bruce was watching Judy now. At all events it looked more like watching to me than like the lover's gaze one might have expected. She seemed aware of his watchfulness and troubled by it, though not profoundly. Exasperated perhaps says a little more accurately what I mean. The brilliant glow of excitement was still in her face, and yet she had fallen silent. Once or twice she darted a quick look at Bill Grant, and at last she may have spoken to him under her breath.

Anyhow I found myself presently watching him, so that I was on the spot, as it were, when his face changed too. It was like the lifting of a fog. I saw him look down the table toward Bruce, and then back at Judy. No, not at Judy; at Judy's necklace. He was staring at it now like one fascinated, and to my amazement his face broke into a broad—but really a ferocious—grin. *His* eyes were blazing now.

I gave up trying to entertain the nice bridesmaid after that. It really didn't matter. She was too excited about the necklace to care.

But for myself, I was in exactly the plight in which old Eagle-Eye had found himself this afternoon. I had seen a drama played out under my eyes, and what it was all about I hadn't the remotest idea. And I went home, once they'd got fairly to dancing, without any further illumination. Judy, as I said, never came near me. Whatever situation she'd foreseen which I might be useful in hadn't come off. She had something else on her mind now.

But this much I knew. Whatever Judy's story might be, the necklace was somehow the nub of it.

CHAPTER XI

WHEN I CAME IN

I got my cue at five minutes past four the next morning. I know what time it was since I had, a moment earlier, switched on my light and looked at my watch to see how much longer the night was going to last. The sky would begin turning gray before very long, I remember thanking heaven, and then perhaps I should drop off to sleep.

It wasn't ten seconds after I'd switched out my light and dropped back upon my pillow, when I heard my name spoken, almost beside my head, it seemed, in a whisper.

I don't mind admitting that if I'd had two practicable legs, I'd have come clean out of bed in one jump. As it was I sat up and took out my suppressed activity in thinking. The name that had been whispered was not the one by which I had been baptized, nor even the familiar nickname which almost everyone calls me by, but a private diminutive which Judy and Punch sometimes used as a mark of affection.

I've been sleeping, since I've been too clumsy to get up and down-stairs on crutches, in a little room on the ground floor which my gardener and his wife used to use for a dining-room. The floor of it is hardly above the ground level, and the open window is low enough for anyone bigger than a child to look through, or for that matter, climb in at. So there was nothing unnatural about the whisper, weird as the effect of it had been.

When it was repeated an instant later, I answered in a low voice, "Come around to the front door and I'll let you in."

I thought it was Punch come down to report some new and exciting development that he couldn't wait till morning to tell me.

Donovan slept up-stairs in a little room over the kitchen, the remotest room in the cottage. I'd had a bell put in to summon him by. My gardener and his wife, who was my cook, had moved out after the fire to the second story of my garage. So if I could move quietly enough not to disturb my nurse, my nocturnal visitor's errand could remain as confidential as he seemed to wish it to be.

I switched on the reading lamp in my living-room as I passed through; then cautiously unlocked and opened the door. Two people were standing on the door-step, but neither of them was the caller I had expected. One of them was Judy, and the other was Bill Grant.

I don't think, though, that I was especially surprised. Down in the bottom of my mind I must have guessed a good deal more, during the past two days, than I had allowed myself to admit. All the same I felt pretty blank for a minute. I just stood there in the doorway and balanced myself upon my crutches. My paralysis seemed to have infected them too, for neither of them moved nor spoke.

At last I said, "You'd better come in."

"Do you want us to?" Judy asked very quietly.

"Yes, of course," I told her, and on the words I swung myself back out of the doorway. "Come into the living-room," I added, "and we'll shut the door, and then perhaps it won't be necessary to let Donovan in on it."

Bill made me follow Judy inside, and it was he who closed both doors— more quietly than I could have done.

I didn't ask what they were doing or were planning to do. There is no mistaking the sort of adventure upon which this pair were about to embark.

"Sit down," I said, "and tell me all about it."

My voice was coming to life a little, but it was hardly satisfactory, even to me, and I wasn't surprised at Judy's question.

"Are you on our side? Because there's no use sitting down and talking unless you are."

I did sit down myself, though, in my easy chair and filled and lighted a pipe before I answered. It was time, not tobacco, that I wanted.

"Of course I'm on your side, Judy," I said at last. "I'll be on any side that I'm satisfied is really yours."

Neither of them had followed my example about sitting down. Young Grant was standing in front of my empty fireplace, his hands behind him— locked together, if I could judge by the tension of his shoulders. Judy, who had been wandering restlessly about the room while I got my pipe going, now gave me a rueful sort of smile and came to rest on the arm of my chair.

"You haven't my best interests at heart, have you?" she asked with slightly burlesqued apprehension. "You don't want to save me from doing something that I'll always regret?"

The words and the manner may have been flippant, but the voice wasn't. Judy trusted me to understand seriousness without the label of a long face, and I blessed her for her confidence in me.

I essayed a small joke of my own. "It's no good your sitting in my lap," I told her. "I'm not old enough to be seduced that way. I want to be satisfied which your side really is, before I fall in, that's all."

"You're absolutely right, sir," said Bill seriously. They were the first words he'd spoken. "You ought to be told the whole story before you're asked to do anything, or even agree to anything."

"No, he's wrong, Bill," Judy contradicted him over my head. (She hadn't stirred, by the way, at my jibe about sitting in my lap.) "He's got to decide first and hear the story afterward. Really the story hasn't a thing to do with it, except that he'll be awfully interested in it—put it in his collection, probably. He knows already, you see, that I mean to marry you and that I'm not going to marry Bruce. Of course, if he thinks that because I'm still rather young I shouldn't be allowed to decide *anything* for myself—which is a mistake that has been made before...."

I saw Bill Grant smile ruefully at that and perceived that he himself had made this mistake.

"... if he does think that," Judy went on, "then, of course, he'll think I'm wrong anyhow, story or no story. But if he thinks I'm grown up, then he'll see that I'm the only person who can possibly know whether you're the man I ought to marry, or Bruce."

"I'll admit that you're grown up, my dear."

She kissed me briefly, and sprang to her feet.

"Well, then, it's like this," she said, turning and facing me very earnestly. "Do you want to get into a whole lot of trouble that you needn't get into at all? Do you want mother to quarrel with you, and grandmother to cut you out of her will, and a whole lot of people to think you've been, well—seduced, you know, into doing something that was perfectly frantically foolish? You needn't, you know. You needn't let any of these things happen. That's why I wanted you to decide first. I wouldn't have you persuaded. But I thought perhaps you'd—just naturally—want to."

I don't know what answer I made; whether, indeed, in words I made any at all. Judy was satisfied at all events, for she went over to her lover, slipped her arm through his, and said, "I knew he would."

Even at that moment I credited this young man with unusually acute perceptions. He made no attempt to express any gratitude of his own, or to speak for Judy in the matter of hers. He'd have annoyed me intensely if he'd done either of these things. What he said was more to the point.

"It may not turn out to be quite so bad as Judy makes it look," he said. "We've a plan that will avoid a general explosion of scandal if it works. It's a near thing, of course, whether it works or not."

"You're an optimist," I commented, "if you think you can run off with Judith Corbin less than twelve hours before she was to have married Bruce Applebury without causing a general explosion of scandal." I was as yet, you see, prepared to be amiable only in streaks.

Judy came back to the arm of my chair and patted me consolingly. "You think so," she said, "because you haven't any idea how clever Bill is. Tell him the plan, Bill," she added.

Young Grant stood very straight, and spoke rather stiffly.

"The essential thing about it is," he said, "that we get married as early as possible this morning, before the people at The Oaks are up and about."

"That's what I told them we were going to do," Judy put in, "in the notes I left—one for mother and one for Bruce. I told mother that by the time she'd read it we'd be married, but if she wanted us to, we'd come back before anybody knew we'd gone and not let on that anything had happened. I left the note in her room so that she'd have time to think before she started anything."

"But the wedding!" I gasped. "The marriage to Bruce in the afternoon! What would you do about that?"

"Oh, they'd have to postpone the wedding," Judy said easily. (I'm not sure she didn't speak through a yawn.) "Get up some excuse. You can trust mother for that. Grandmother could be horribly ill. That would be easiest, of course. The people would all go away, don't you see, and then when they'd stopped thinking about us, Bill and I could be married again. There's no law against that, is there?"

"But why be married now?" I asked. "Why not simply postpone the wedding? The same excuse would serve."

"Tell him, Bill," commanded Judy.

"I know Bruce pretty well," young Grant said, "and I imagine Judy knows her mother. I don't believe either of them would submit quietly to anything less than the proved inevitable. And unless they made up their minds to it instantly and put the excuse over—for all they were worth—it wouldn't be any good. If they know there's nothing left to argue about, they may plant their excuse at once and send for us."

"Send for you where?" I asked.

Judy gave a guilty sort of wriggle.

"I had to let you in for it, a little," she said. "I told mother that as soon as we were married, we would let you know where we were, and that if she wanted us to come back, she was to call up your house and find out."

"Where *will* you be?" I asked.

Judy didn't answer. She left my chair again and walked away, but not, this time, to where her lover was standing; there was a moment before she turned and faced me.

"Do you *want* to get into this?" she demanded of me. She was intensely serious now. "It will be beastly for you. Mother will hate you, whether the plan works and they save their faces or not. We didn't want to do it this way, you know. At least, Bill didn't. We wouldn't have done it if we could have helped it. I can't marry anyone else but Bill—not now, and they—they haven't left us any way but this. But you don't deserve to be—to be made the goat."

I'd never seen tears in Judy's eyes before, but they were there now, and they brought a responsive blur into my own.

"I shall enjoy being the goat," I said, "and I'll double in any other useful part that you can assign to me. How about it? Will you be married here?"

Judy heaved a deep sigh of assent. "In this nice little house," she said. She turned to her lover. "It's all right now, Bill."

Bill Grant came over and shook hands with me.

"I can't tell you what a relief it is, sir," he said. "I didn't want to take Judy on a wild goose chase through the middle of the night looking for a license clerk and a justice of the peace. I wanted it known where she was. If I may leave her here with you, I'll drive over now to the county-seat and get a license as soon as I can wake up the clerk."

"I'll keep Judy for you," I said. "But there's no use in your starting yet. It's only a twenty-mile drive, and you can't rout that man out in the middle of the night. Sit down and be comfortable."

"Do you keep anything to eat in your house?" Judy asked. "I'm hungry, now that I can think about something besides eloping with Bill."

I told her where to find the ice-box, and cautioned her to go quietly in order not to waken Donovan. Bill went with her, and they came back in a few minutes with three-quarters of a pie, and a bottle of milk. We set out the feast on the little table beside my couch, and I watched them eat, mercifully refraining from asking any questions. These babes in the wood were as hungry as the wolves that would have devoured them.

But when we'd finished, and when Bill Grant and I had lighted our pipes, I asked, "Now, haven't I earned the story for my collection? When did you two youngsters meet for the first time? Yesterday afternoon?"

Judy curled up on my couch, happy as a well-fed kitten.

"Tell him about it, Bill," she said. "I think I'm going to sleep. The whole works, you know," she continued. And by way of launching him she spoke once more to me.

"Has mother told you about my horrible past? Well, Bill's it!"

CHAPTER XII

AN EXCURSION INTO ARCADY

Of course I knew what Judy meant by her horrible past. The escapade Victoria had told me about while she was trying to persuade me to help her put the soft pedal on Alexander Corbin's activities in the matter of the theft of the necklace. She hadn't, to be sure, so much told me about it, as bounded it for me. It began, I knew, in Judy's flight from school and ended in the Martha Washington Hotel where Victoria had found her, "looking as if she hadn't found liberty as jolly as she'd expected."

The natural inference from this last remark of Judy's was that it was Bill Grant who had disillusioned her, who had reduced her to that cynical acquiescence in defeat which I'd found it so hard to understand in her. The appropriate thing for me to have done then, under the traditional code, would have been to tell the young man he was a yellow dog and order him out of my house. But the notion of doing anything like that was so absurd that I smiled at him.

Bill misunderstood the smile.

"It's quite true, sir," he said soberly.

"He knows it's true," Judy remarked.

"You go to sleep," he told her gently, "and don't listen in. I want to tell this my own way."

But it seemed he couldn't begin. He sat there taking his pipe in short, sharp little puffs, his eyes unfocused, his thoughts astray all over the area of the past. He seemed to be exploring for a path that would take him through.

"To begin with," I said at last, to help him out, "tell me who you are."

"Well, I *am* Bruce Applebury's cousin," he answered doubtfully.

"I don't mean that," I said.

"Tell him what you do," put in Judy.

"Shut up," he ordered, "and go to sleep."

"I'm not an Applebury," he then said to me, possessed of the thread at last. "His mother and mine are sisters. Osborne, their name was. We don't see them much. Father, mother and I have traveled around a good deal—a little like Henry James' family, though I don't mean the results have been the same. Anyhow, until I went to college, my education had been a catch-as-catch-can affair, never in one school very long. Bruce, of course, did every-thing perfectly regularly, so I didn't see so very much of him. And after we graduated and he went into the family bank, I saw him still less. I really know him pretty well, though, and that's important."

I could see that it might be, but I wasn't ready to go back to Bruce. I remembered Judy's comment, "Tell him what you do," so now I asked him.

"Oh," he said, embarrassed, "I try to write."

"What do you write?" I asked.

"Why, I've tried my hand at pretty nearly everything but poetry," he told me. "When I met Judy, down in Easton, Pennsylvania, I was traveling around on a try-out circuit, one-night stands mostly, with a play of mine, trying to lick it into shape, as they say, and hoping it would get into New York. It never did. It died out on the road. But I wasn't there when it happened. I left it in Easton."

"Where you met Judy?" I suggested.

"Yes," he admitted. "But not because I'd met her. I'd already made up my mind to quit when that happened. I'd come to hate the thing so that it made me sick. Every change they made in it made it worse, until I hoped it would die on the road. If it had ever got in New York, I'd have run like a rabbit."

"Anyhow you *did* meet Judy," I persisted. "How did it happen?"

Once more his face was shiny with sweat, and he mopped it with his handkerchief.

"Oh, it sounds rotten," he said miserably. "You'll think I ought to be kicked, and I wouldn't deny it. But then, you know Judy. You *do* know her, don't you?" he shot at me fiercely.

"Yes, I know her," I said. "Go on."

"She was a waitress in the hotel," he resumed. "One of these coffee-shop places, you know, where half the town comes for lunch. I talked to her over a meal or two. She'd been to see my play. One night I overtook her on the street, and instead of going to that damned theater, I went for a long walk with her.

"Of course I'd known from the first word she spoke to me that she wasn't an ordinary waitress.... Well—naturally. But I couldn't make her out at all. She wouldn't tell me anything about herself. She gave me a name to call her by, but she told me while we were on that walk that it wasn't hers.

"By way of playing the game I didn't tell her anything about myself, ei-ther. She knew my name, of course, but I let her think it was a *nom de plume*. It was Osborne Grant on the programs, and I told her to call me Bill. It got to be a sort of understanding that we took each other as is, without explanations.

"You can't imagine what it was like. Well, perhaps you can, but I'd never imagined that anything like that could happen. It was the only really romantic thing that ever had happened to me. And it was like that from the very first moment.

"On that walk we took I told her I was going to quit the play. I said I was so deadly sick of it that I couldn't go on with it. I said I was going to buy a Ford and go somewhere, disappear for a while—get lost.

"It's hard to be sure you're being honest telling about a thing like that. I suppose I must have had it in the back of my head as an awfully jolly possibility that she'd come with me. We talked about it at first as a joke, and then she said to me suddenly, 'Are you really joking? Because if you aren't, I'll come.' She said she was on a sort of tramp, anyhow. She meant to work her way west, clear to the Pacific coast perhaps."

He broke off and looked at her. She was sound asleep now, and no mistake. He went to the couch and drew a light blanket over her.

"She's had a rotten two days," he said, as he stood looking down at her. Then he went back to his chair.

"You'll find it hard to believe, sir," he went on. "I find it hard myself to believe it now. She looks like a little girl, asleep there. But I really thought, then, that she was as old as I was. She seemed harder. She seemed to have seen a lot of life. I don't know how she could put it on. It was a sort of defensive armor, I suppose. Anyhow, I didn't feel I was taking any advantage of her. And I didn't expect to be any Sir Galahad about it, either. I don't know that I exactly expected the other thing. I was just willing to let it ride. I'd only just begun to know her then, you see.

"Well, I bought a Ford, and she quit her job and we started out. And on that first day together I began to see what she was really like. She kept getting younger, and, well—I don't know any other word—sweeter; taking off the armor, you know, as she tried me out and came to feel I was all right.

"We went across Pennsylvania, through Lancaster and Gettysburg, and hit the old National Trail in Maryland; followed it up into the Cumberland Mountains. We didn't get on very fast, because whenever we saw anything we thought it would be jolly to stop and do—nice little brooks to wade in; things like that—we stopped and did it.

"I did turn out to be, well—a Galahad, after all, though it wasn't any merit of mine. The thing just took itself for granted, the first time we put up for the night. I won't talk any brother and sister rot. No brother and sister ever were like that. But we always slept in separate rooms. We didn't pay any attention to appearances, though. If the rooms happened to be adjoining, it was all the better. We talked through the door.

"That lasted a week. And then I couldn't trust myself any further. We were in love with each other, you see. Oh, we'd been that from the first, but now each of us knew the other knew it. You know what *she's* like. She'd never welsh in her life. She'd go through with anything that she started; perfectly reckless, if no one but herself was concerned.

"Well, that was all right. We might have got married then and there, and it would have saved a terrible lot of anguish if we had. But by that time I'd come to. I knew how young she was—she'd given that away—and I knew she was a runaway. She'd never told me her name, nor what her people were like. I knew what they must be like, of course.

"Well, it struck me that I couldn't look them in the face, nor Judy, nor even myself, if I took advantage of a child's escapade like that. I hadn't any idea of giving her up, but I thought I'd figured out a way to square the thing. I wrote her a letter, and slipped it under her door that last night, and bolted. It seemed the right thing to do, but I knew by instinct I was being a fool all the time.

"I told her in the letter that I loved her, and always would, but that I wanted her to go home to her own people and her own surroundings and take a little while to think it over. I said that after she had thought it over she was to make her choice.

"I said it was perfectly possible that when she found herself back among her old friends, she'd think of this adventure of ours as something perfectly insane. If it did seem like that she wasn't to worry. I'd never try to follow her up, and she could remember it as a pleasant episode. Lord, what a fool I was! I might have known how Judy would take that.

"I went on to tell her of course, that I loved her as I never would love anything else in the world, and if she found she still loved me, back home with her feet on the ground, she was to write me a letter and I'd come like a shot. I signed it with my full name, of course, and wrote out my permanent address. And then I wrote a postscript telling her she wasn't to have any regrets whichever way she decided it, because she'd given me something....

"Well, you know how it is, sir. It looked all right on the page. I thought I meant it; meant that I could be satisfied with what I'd had, even if it stopped there. Of course I was a perfectly doddering fool.

"Oh, and I did one more fool thing. I didn't know how her money was holding out. I was afraid she might be completely strapped. So I put a couple of twenty-dollar bills in the envelope to pay her fare home.

"I drove off in the night, and I turned back three times before morning. I wish to God I'd gone all the way back, but I never did. I hung on, somehow, to my fool idea.

"Well, of course I began watching for a letter from her within a week. I didn't know her handwriting nor what the postmark would be, and every time I found a letter addressed in a woman's handwriting, my heart stopped beating—literally stopped, I mean, for one beat anyhow, and there isn't a thing the matter with it.

"After three months of that I was pretty nearly crazy. I couldn't go looking for her, you see. I'd sawed myself off that limb by promising her that I wouldn't. I couldn't be sure she hadn't taken me at my word; decided she'd done a perfectly crazy thing—which it was, of course, by all her home standards—and was only hoping that I'd never turn up to remind her of it. My mother saw I was half out of my head about something, and persuaded me finally to go to Italy with her for the rest of the winter. I made extra careful arrangements for my mail to be forwarded, and went.

"I came back just in time for Bruce to ask me to be best man at his wedding. I was a little surprised at his doing that, because we've never been friends really, but he's great on family, and going out, as it seemed to him, into the wilds like this, he wanted to rally us around and present a united front. I agreed to it, of course. I'd nothing else to do.

"He didn't talk about her much; never showed me her picture. Well, he wouldn't. I hadn't had the slightest warning, not a hint, when I got out of that car under the porte-cochère at The Oaks and saw her standing there in the veranda."

I had paid his tale the tribute of almost breathless attention, and even now when he paused as if he'd come to the end of it, it was a good while before I could find anything to say.

At last I asked a question. "Why didn't Judy write to you?"

"She'd torn up my letter in a rage before she'd ever got as far as my name and address at the bottom of it. Oh, naturally enough. Think of the perfectly hellish jolt she must have got just from the sight of those two damned twenty-dollar bills, and the knowledge that I'd gone!

"And the thing I'd really done wasn't very much better. Do you remember what she said just now, about thinking she was too young to be allowed to decide anything for herself? That was the theory I'd gone on. I'd taken the decision out of her hands."

"It was the chivalrous thing to do," I argued dubiously, but wasn't very much surprised when he flung the word back at my head.

"Oh, chivalry be damned! She deserved to have been taken in on it, all right, and I ought to have known it. Lord, I'd had seven solid days of her. She hadn't acted like a silly kid out for a lark. I was a coward, that's what it came to. I was afraid if I told her what my plan was that she'd talk me out of it and I'd cave in and be left looking like a crook. Hell, there are times when a man ought to have courage enough to *be* a crook!

"But I wasn't at the end of my chivalry yet, even when I saw her there at The Oaks Thursday afternoon, saw her turn white and bolt into the house, and found out she was the girl that Bruce was going to marry.

"I saw through the sprained ankle dodge, of course, and decided I wouldn't play tennis. I was hanging around the hall waiting for a sight of her, when Punch caught me and showed me to my room. I did have a few minutes with her afterward, when the others were out on the courts.

"But I was still trying not to look like a crook. I started out by trying to tell her she needn't be afraid, that I hadn't known I'd find her here and that I wouldn't give her away. Oh, I don't blame myself so much for that. I was rattled, naturally. But I'd lost my chance for a talk that would get anywhere with her, and it began to look as if I'd never have another.

"By the time that first infernal evening was half over (lord, it was only night before last) I was desperate. I went off up-stairs and sat down and wrote her another letter. She'd told me why she hadn't written me, so I had that much to go on. And of course I knew without any question at all, that, regardless of what happened to me, she ought never to marry Bruce.

"It would be a perfect crime, a marriage like that, for Judy. Bruce isn't a monster, nor a villain, nor anything like that. But he's stiff and self-satisfied, and bull-headed, and he hasn't the imagination of a good Ford car. He'd try to break Judy on the wheel without knowing he was doing it.

"I don't think he *could* break her, but he might drive her to almost anything. Well, I put all of that and a whole lot besides, into that letter, and then went out on the veranda where she was sitting and handed it to her."

"I'll tell the world he did," came a sleepy voice from the couch. "I could have killed him. He explained afterward he thought I could tuck it in my dress."

"Well," I asked, "why didn't you?"

She opened her eyes and looked at me with a hopeless expression.

"What do you think we wear?" she asked me. "Corsets? All I had on, that night, besides my shoes and stockings was a shirt and a step-in—and my dress, of course. Where do you think the letter would have stopped if I'd stuck it down inside?"

It came as a shock to me to realize that this time-honored repository, consecrated by tradition to the implements of intrigue, love-notes, keep-sakes, and so on, had become as obsolete as a sedan chair, but there was no getting away from the logic of the facts.

Judy, still curled up on the couch, was broad awake now, and went on telling me about it.

"I saw Bruce bearing down on me, so I shoved the letter down into that silly Chinese vase that people are always dropping cigarettes into, although I knew I'd have a fearful time getting it out. If I could have been sure what line Bill had taken in his letter I'd have hung on to it and seen the thing through with Bruce then and there. But I had to read it first. So I climbed out of my window in the middle of the night and got it and read it, and then spent the rest of the time until daylight riding around on Punch's bicycle, deciding what I'd do.

"Poor little Punch! I wouldn't have cared except that he saw the whole thing. He saw me hide the letter in the first place, and he knew when I went out to get it. I don't know what he thought."

"I can guess what he thought," I said. "He thought it had something to do with the loss and the return of the necklace. That's what I'd have thought too, if he'd told me about it. Now it seems that the necklace had nothing to do, from start to finish, with the whole affair."

They looked at me and looked at each other. Bill drew a long, heart-felt sigh of dissent.

"Hadn't it just!" he said. "It was that infernal necklace that made all the trouble, really."

CHAPTER XIII

STUNG!

I saw, though, by the way he pulled himself up, that he wasn't going to tell me about it; not then, anyhow. He walked to the window, and then looked at his watch.

"I'm off," he said decisively. "It's almost broad daylight now, and I don't want to waste any time getting things started."

"You can't get a public official out of bed in any such ungodly hour as this," I protested.

But he was oddly determined about it.

"I can keep on trying till I do," he assured me.

So I gave over the ungrateful rôle of obstructionist and started in to help.

"You'll want a parson as well as a license," I pointed out, and named a man who I thought might be willing to serve. "He's quite a nice young chap, new here in the village. He's been out to see me three or four times since I've been laid up—out of pure amiability, nothing professional about it—and we've become pretty good friends. I'll give you a card to him. You can tell him your story, and if he wants any confirmation that I can give him, he can call me up. He won't mind getting up early, so on your way back with the license you can stop and bring him along. You've a car, haven't you?"

"Quite a good one," said Judy. "I don't know whose it is."

Bill looked a little startled at that. Then he grinned. "Oh well," he said, "what's one small sport roadster among friends? I'll bring it back all right."

Judy went, but no farther than the door, to see him off.

"You know, I like Bill," she said, in the thoughtful manner of one announcing a discovery, when she came back into my sitting-room. And she wouldn't agree, when I laughed, that there was anything funny about it.

"It's an entirely different thing from being in love with him," she insisted. "He's got what they used to call—in old-fashioned novels, you know—delicacy. I'm sure I know why he was in such a hurry to get off. It was because we'd got around to the necklace, and he doesn't like to talk about it. He didn't want to hear me tell you about it, and he knew I was going to. It is a dirty sort of story, of course, but—well, there it is. You want me to tell you about it, don't you?"

"Lord, *yes*!" I cried. Really, I don't like whitewash much better than she does. I added, "I could hardly bear it yesterday when old Mr. Smith came back to the summer-house and kept you from telling it then."

"I didn't know it, then," she said. "Not the worst of it. The real worst of it hadn't happened.

"You know I told you—when was it, Wednesday morning when I came over here?—what a jolt mother had got over the newspaper story that Gran was going to give me the necklace? Well, that night, just before dinner, after Gran had told her that she really was going to give it to me, mother told me that she was in trouble about it.

"You see, about a year ago, Gran had given her the necklace to take to town to the jeweler to be cleaned and restrung, and mother had had an imitation necklace made then. She told me she'd done it because the real one was likely to be stolen any time out of that silly old safe Gran kept it in, especially now that she was taking so much dope and forgot to lock it half the time. She put the real one in the bank, she said, where it would be safe, and brought the imitation back to grandmother. It got by with Gran, all right. She never suspected a thing.

"But she told me if Gran did give it to me for a wedding present it was likely to be found out that it was an imitation. What she wanted to do was to go back to town next day and get the real one out of the bank and put it back in the safe, instead of the imitation, so that Gran shouldn't know that an imitation had been made. If Gran ever found that out, she said, there was no telling what she'd do. She'd probably disinherit Punch and me by way of getting even with mother, especially after Uncle Alec had come back and made up their quarrel.

"Even if she didn't do that, mother said, Gran would be sure to make a perfectly frightful row and accuse her of having tried to steal the necklace, which would be pretty rotten right in the middle of the wedding, with the Appleburys there and all.

"Mother said it was harder to get the necklace out of the bank than it had been to put it in. There were more formalities about it, especially since it had come out in the paper that Gran was going to give it to me. Mother wanted me to write a note, to show to the bank, saying that Gran had given me the necklace and that they were to let mother take it out.

"I didn't want to do that because she hadn't given it to me, and I didn't more than half believe she really would. I didn't believe that until last night when she did. She'd promised to give it to mother a dozen times.

"Mother and I rather quarreled about that. But at last we made it up. She said she'd go and try to get the bank to give her the necklace anyhow without any note from me, but that if she didn't get it and Gran did give the imitation to me, I was to take it and hand it right over to her; refuse to wear it, you know, and not give anybody a chance to look at it, not even Bruce, and especially not old Mr. Smith whom grandmother said she'd invited to the wedding. Because, of course, he'd spot it for an imitation in a minute.

"I was glad enough to agree to that. I didn't want to wear the beastly thing. Mother went back to town Thursday morning to try to get the bank to give her the necklace, but didn't succeed.

"Well, and then Bill came the same afternoon and I forgot all about the necklace. He'd driven me pretty nearly wild in that first little talk with him. The only question I wanted to decide was whether it would be better to run away then and there with Bill, or to stay and go through with the program, only marry Bill instead of Bruce when the time came. Bill didn't see it that way at all. He was still being—chivalrous, you know, like he said.

"So when grandmother sent for me to try on the necklace and there was nothing there but that silly empty box, it struck me as rather funny. I shouldn't have laughed, of course.

"It seemed such an ideal way of settling mother's troubles that I wanted to let it ride, just as she did. We didn't care whether Gran had hidden it somewhere and forgotten, or whether it had really been stolen. If it had, it was a joke on the thief, that's all. All we wanted was to keep Uncle Alec from sending for the police, which would have made a lot of trouble, especially if they got it back and found it was only an imitation after all. Well, you got him quieted down, and that seemed to be all right.

"I read Bill's letter by the light of Punch's bicycle lantern that night and saw that he felt the same way that I did about everything. He didn't want me to marry Bruce, anyhow. All we needed was a good long talk, which might be rather hard to manage, of course, and we'd work everything out.

"Then, awfully early yesterday morning, mother came in in her nightgown, half wild, to tell me that the imitation necklace had turned up again in grandmother's room, and that Mr. Smith was coming that morning. She accused Punch of having taken it, and called him a little fiend for bringing it back.

"She came back about an hour later, though, a whole lot calmer and said she'd got everything fixed up. Bruce was going into town, she said, to get the necklace. He'd told her how to work it and she'd given him the sort of note the bank wanted. He'd be back with it on the three o'clock train in time for the rehearsal.

"She wanted me to get up and dress right away and drive Bruce to the station, but not go in town with him because he'd be awfully busy and I'd be in his way. She told me not to say anything to him about the necklace. She wanted the crowd to think I'd gone in with him, though, so that his going off like that wouldn't look queer. I was to keep out of sight wherever I pleased till it was time for his train to come back. And she said she'd fixed Mr. Smith so that he wouldn't come to the house till dinner tonight.

"Well, of course it would have looked fishy to me if I'd thought about it at all. But the only thing I thought of was that here was a perfectly heaven-sent chance for my talk with Bill. So I sent a note up to him and told him where to meet me.

"We went up to the summer-house, thinking it would be the safest place there was, and found you there with old Mr. Smith. He'd seen us through his field-glasses, of course, and we must have given him something to think about. But it didn't seem to matter much then. We got away as soon as we could and had our talk.

"Bill was stubborn about it. He wouldn't hear of my marrying him, then. The only thing to do, he said, was to call off the marriage with Bruce. He wanted that and my marriage to him, he said, to be two separate things. I told him he wanted to be sure he wasn't getting me on the rebound. But of course that wasn't fair. I can really see how it looked to him. He's—well, he's like that.

"So what we agreed on was that I was to meet Bruce at the three o'clock train and drive him around a while before we came back to The Oaks and tell him that I wasn't going to marry him; I'd do anything else he wanted, except that. He could throw me over any way he liked, tell any story he wanted to tell. If he wanted the thing done quietly, I'd pretend to be awfully ill, or grandmother could, and the wedding could be postponed.

"It was a perfectly rotten position to put him in, and it wasn't his fault that he was in it—at least it wasn't his fault any more than it was mine. I'd never told him I was in love with him. I had told him when he first asked me to marry him that I'd been in love with someone else, but I said I didn't know where he was and that he was out of my life altogether. Of course I thought that was true. He said he'd take a chance. Well, I was going to have to tell him that the chance turned out to be that the man had come back, neither by his fault nor mine, and that we were in love with each other. It never struck me as possible that Bruce would want to marry me when he knew that. You wouldn't think it was possible, would you?"

"Yes, my dear," I told her regretfully, "I'm afraid I would."

"Well," she conceded, "you know more about life than I do.

"I met him and we drove off down the Yorkville Road, and I told him the whole thing. He didn't say a word; just sat there looking blacker and blacker every minute till I'd finished. And then the horrible thing happened.

"He told me he'd been stung. He told me what had really happened about the necklace. And the minute he began talking I knew it was true. He told me mother had really taken it—he used perfectly horrible words: 'fraudulently hypothecated it.' That means she'd pretended it was hers and got the bank to let her have some money on it; a lot of money—twenty-five thousand dollars. She'd tried to raise the money to get it back and she couldn't. And when they found out that the necklace wasn't hers they'd threatened her, Bruce said, with a criminal prosecution. Of course she was almost crazy with worry about it. So she'd gone to *him*, to *Bruce*, and asked him to put up the money to get the necklace back."

That was more than I could listen to in silence.

"She went to Bruce!" I cried. "Good God!"

"I suppose she couldn't think of anyone else to go to," Judy said thoughtfully. "It had to be someone she could absolutely count on to keep it quiet. He'd hate a scandal in his family worse than anything else in the world, and of course mother thought, and so did he, that I was as good as married to him.

"But when he had paid the money to the bank and got the necklace, and then found I didn't mean to marry him, he felt that he'd been, as he said, stung. Even the necklace wasn't his, he said. It was practically stolen goods. It had belonged to grandmother all the time. She could have made the bank give it back to her without paying back the money, just by proving to them that mother hadn't had any right to give it to them.

"Oh, I can see now how he felt about it. I suppose for anyone like him it was the natural way to feel. But I couldn't see anything then. I'd just gone dead, like a flat tire.

"We went along for miles after he'd told me that nice little story without saying a word, either of us. Then I told him I'd marry him if he wanted me to. I said it seemed that I'd already been sold to him. I couldn't see any other way out. I couldn't pay him his beastly twenty-five thousand dollars, and I didn't know anyone I could ask for it—not for a thing like that.

"I didn't begin to hate him till then. I'd hated myself, and hated mother. But when I told him I'd marry him because he'd paid me— Oh, I told him more than that too. I said that he could do anything he liked with me, but that I loved Bill and would go right on loving him. And after I'd told him all that, he began to get—*amiable*.

"He said he'd known he could trust me to do the right thing. He'd been sure all the time I hadn't known what mother had asked him to do. He said it was a foolish fancy that I was in love with Bill. That I'd get over it as soon as we'd been married a little while. He said he was acting for my own good and what I needed now was a little firmness to keep me from leaving the rails and making a hash of my whole life. He said he was sure we were going to be happy together.

"I didn't say anything at all; just hung on and kept from jumping out of the car. That's how we got back to The Oaks.

"Of course the minute Bill saw the satisfied look in Bruce's face he knew I'd fallen down on him somehow. It wasn't the sort of thing he'd expected me to do, and he was pretty well upset. So after the rehearsal I took him off in front of everybody and told him what had happened. I didn't have time for the details, of course, but I told him Bruce had paid for me in advance.

"He wanted me to postpone the wedding, anyhow, and give him time to raise the money himself. I told him I wasn't going to be auctioned off any more, let alone to him. He says now that he saw the point all right, but he wouldn't admit it then. The last thing he said was that he'd think of a way yet, and I told him it was all right if he could. He's terribly clever, but I don't believe there was any way, except the one that happened."

"What did happen?" I asked. I'll admit my mind wasn't working very well. It was too boiling hot.

"Why," she cried, "you were there! You saw it happen. Gran gave me the necklace, right before everybody. Didn't you hear me ask her if it was *really* mine, and hear her say it was? It was only the imitation one, of course, but she thought it was the real one. The real one was right in Bruce's pocket where it belonged. So all I had to do was to tell him to keep the necklace. That's what I said in my note to him. And poor old Bill didn't see it for about five minutes after it happened."

There wasn't much to say after that. I could see how horribly tired she was—could anyone wonder?—and I suggested presently that she go back to my couch and take another nap while we waited for Bill to come with the parson and the license. She took to the suggestion readily.

"We're supposed to be pretty wild," she observed, referring, I suppose, to her generation, "but I don't believe we like it quite as wild as this. It's over, anyhow. There isn't anything more that can happen now."

With that, being the perfectly healthy young animal that she was, she fell contentedly asleep.

I'm not so young and my nerves don't bear stretching so easily. So for a good while I sat watching her, thinking over the story she'd told me, fitting it in with what I'd already known of the queer series of happenings which had so disturbed and mystified me during the past three days.

I had it all now, hadn't I? Well no, not quite. I didn't know yet who'd stolen the imitation necklace in the first place and then incomprehensibly brought it back. It didn't matter much, though, did it? Old Eagle-Eye thought it did. Probably old Mrs. Corbin herself had mislaid the necklace or hidden it somewhere, perhaps under the influence of her drug, and under the same influence, restored it, the way it happened in *The Moonstone*.

Yes, but how about Punch's man in pajamas?—Oh, well, Punch might have dreamed him.

With dreams in my mind I must have fallen asleep myself, just then, in my chair.

What wakened me was the persistent ringing of a telephone bell. It hadn't wakened Judy, so I hobbled over to the instrument as quickly as I could and answered it.

"This is Alexander Corbin," I heard the voice say. "I'm afraid I've wakened you. I want to tell you that Bruce Applebury was robbed last night of the Corbin necklace."

"Robbed!" I repeated stupidly. "How?"

"He tells a very queer story. He came to my room with it just now. I'll give you the details later. I'm talking on Victoria's phone. She wants me to ask whether you happen to know anything of the whereabouts of young William Grant?"

"Not precisely," I said. "I can give you some news of him, though. Shall I come up to The Oaks?"

"I wish to heaven you would!" Alec exclaimed. "And the quicker you get here, the better."

CHAPTER XIV

A POINT OF HONOR

I heard a sudden move from Judy on the couch and looked around at her. She was sitting bolt upright, gazing at me wide-eyed.

"Has something happened to Bill?" she asked.

"No, it's Bruce," I said. "He was robbed of the necklace last night."

"But why did you say anything about Bill?" she persisted.

"Your mother wanted to know whether I could tell them where he was. It was Alec who talked to me."

She was still looking rather wild-eyed, like one under some nightmare apprehension. Indeed I thought the shadows of the sleep she'd just awakened from must still be clouding her mind a little. The fact was, of course, that she was thinking straighter and faster than I.

"Which necklace do you suppose it was," I asked, "that Bruce was robbed of; the real one or the imitation?"

"The real one, of course," she said. "It's the only one he had. He brought it home from the bank, you see, and when mother couldn't get the imitation away from Gran, in order to put the real one in place of it, Bruce said he thought it would be safer if he kept it and if nobody knew he had it. Nobody did know he had it but mother and me." She made a full stop there. Then, "And Bill," she added. "Of course I told him."

She swung her legs off the couch as if about to spring to her feet, but arrested the action half-completed. She was thinking, I could see, with an agonized intensity, and I found myself now upon the trail of her thoughts.

"Your mother must have read your note," I observed. "That's why she had Alec ask me if I knew where Bill was. You wrote a note to Bruce, too, didn't you? How did you deliver that one?"

"I had Bill take it into his room," she said, "after he'd gone to sleep. That's what we waited for. That's why we were so late getting away."

It's Judy's order that this story isn't to be a whitewash, so I must in common honesty forbear to apply the brush to myself.

I didn't, even for one grisly moment, believe that Bill was the thief; that his elopement with Judy had been a mere pretext and that he was speeding away now to parts unknown with the necklace in his pocket. But I perceived the plausibility of the pattern his actions made.

It wasn't merely that he had known Bruce had the necklace, that he'd gone to Bruce's room when Bruce was asleep, and that he and the necklace were now gone. There were some queerly confirmatory details. He hadn't been willing to consider eloping with Judy until he knew Bruce had the necklace. He had been at some pains to leave Judy in my hands as soon as possible after they'd got out of the house. It had struck me that he'd been rather unreasonably in a hurry to set out on his quest of the license clerk. He'd shown a dislike of hearing the necklace discussed; had run away—this was Judy's own explanation—from hearing her story of its adventures.

I didn't believe that any of this nightmare nonsense really explained anything, but I did find myself wishing, with a kind of prayerful intensity, that he would come back now with his parson and his license. How long had he been gone? What time was it anyhow? By the clock on the mantelpiece it was quarter to seven.

"Look here, Judy," I said. "I told Alec I'd come right up to The Oaks, and I'll go as soon as I can dress and get up there in my car. But there's no reason why this should interfere with your plans."

She looked at me in pitiful bewilderment.

"What are my plans?" she said. "I don't know what you mean."

"Your plans for getting married to Bill," I explained. "You wait here till he comes back with the license and the minister. Get Donovan and the gardener and his wife for your witnesses. Go ahead and marry Bill. And then—well, do just as you like. Start off on your wedding journey, or else stay here. After I've seen how the situation looks at The Oaks, I can telephone to you, if you'd like me to, and you can come back just as you had planned, and pretend that nothing has happened. I didn't tell Alec you were here. All I said was that I could give some news of Bill."

"I can't be married to Bill now," she said. "Not till Bruce has got the necklace back."

I started to say that I didn't see the connection, but she broke in upon me with a savage intensity.

"Don't you see, it's the necklace that bought me off. Mother bargained me for it, and I gave it to him and got clear. Now he hasn't got it. It's been taken away from him. And I can't marry Bill till he's got it back. I'm—I'm caught in a trap."

And indeed, her eyes had the panic in them that I've seen once or twice, in those of a trapped animal. It was unbearable to see little Judy looking like that.

"Let's try to keep our feet on the ground," I said, "and see where we really stand.

"You gave those pearls to Bruce in good faith. You told him in the note that they were his. That lets you out. Suppose he hadn't been robbed of them last night but were to have his pocket picked of them tomorrow in town. You wouldn't feel that bound you to turn yourself over to him. Well, what's the difference?

"Neither you nor Bill had anything to do with the robbery. You *know* Bill didn't. You know that from no conceivable motive, sordid or other, would Bill touch that necklace. He'd have done anything to defend Bruce's possession of it, for it was his release as much as it was yours."

I saw tears spring into her eyes and she came over to me, kissed me briefly, and went back to the couch. "There are two of us, then," she said, "—and I guess there's Punch; that makes three."

She was counting up, I knew, the people who were on her side.

"And old Mr. Smith," I added. "I think you can count him in."

She looked a little surprised at that and I went on:

"Not for any emotional reason. Simply because he's so damned intelligent. The advantage of knowing as an axiom that Bill was not the thief is that we can count intelligence on our side."

I couldn't feel that this had impressed her very much, but she was quieter anyhow, and she was giving me a hearing.

"And it seems to me," I went on, "that another advantage of our certainty of Bill is that it makes it possible for you to marry him first and tackle the problem of the necklace afterward."

She smiled at that. "Bill wouldn't marry me even if I asked him. And I won't ask him. I should, of course, if I were a little bit in doubt about him, or if I were afraid he'd think I was. But we aren't like that. We're— Oh, you can't talk about it. Look: you know what it's been like at home, don't you, ever since—well, ever since father died? Even Punch has hated it, and it hasn't been so bad for him because he can't remember father. And they treat a girl worse anyhow.

"I've never been educated. I don't know anything. I've been *trained*. When father owned a racing stable he used to breed race horses. Well, I've been brought up like that. I hated it so that at last I ran away.

"But I didn't know *why* I hated it until I met Bill. Of course I've known honorable people before, but never anyone that I'd had a chance to see all the way through. It's different, and it's going to be different. When I go with him I'm not going to take any of mother's—bargains along with me."

I've never been very enthusiastic about Victoria, but I felt that I had to come to her defense here.

"I'm not in your mother's confidence," I said to Judy, "but there's something I don't think we can lose sight of. Victoria's had a pretty rotten time herself since your father died. She's got a small income of her own and she could have been comfortable and independent on it if she'd been willing to give in to your grandmother's ideas about bringing up you two children. They may have been better ideas than her own, but she didn't think they were. She took on what's turned out to be a long battle, as she saw it in your behalf. If she got herself into money difficulties so desperate that she was driven to hypothecate the necklace, she did it so that she could give you what she regarded as a fair chance."

"I'm glad you told me that," Judy said, after a moment of blank silence. "At least I think I am. But you see it ties me down all the tighter. I've got to keep her bargain—one way or the other."

"You don't mean," I cried, "that you'd marry Bruce *now*!"

She nodded.

"But I'm not going to do it," she said. "We're going back to The Oaks and find that necklace. You ring for Donovan to come down and help you dress. I'll leave a note for Bill, and then I'll go up to the garage and get out your car."

CHAPTER XV

BLACK LOOKS

We made up for lost time once we got started. It wasn't much after half past seven when we got to The Oaks. Alec was waiting to let us in, and he was flabbergasted at the sight of Judy. Evidently Victoria hadn't been giving out any more information than she considered necessary. He started two or three exclamatory interrogations, but left them all in the air. He probably realized that a thorough answer to any question would take longer than he had time for just then.

Judy asked him, "Where's Bruce?"

"He's with your mother up in her sitting-room," Alec told her.

At that Judy went straight into the house, leaving him to accompany my slower progress on my crutches.

"I think Victoria is mad," he told me confidentially. "The necklace is gone, and she won't let me make any move toward finding it. Applebury seems to believe that his cousin has levanted with it, and if that's so, it's perhaps a case for negotiation rather than for ordinary police methods. But to me that theory seems fantastic. Don't you agree with me?"

"Absolutely," I said. "I'd be willing to bet all I've got that Bill Grant hasn't stolen the necklace."

"Then, in heaven's name," he implored me, "convince Victoria if you can that the thing to do is to commence a search—discover if any of the servants have disappeared. If this were my house I'd put a cordon of the farm laborers around it and not let anyone get out until we'd had time to satisfy ourselves that the necklace wasn't inside."

By that time he had run me up in the elevator and piloted me to Victoria's door.

"No, I'm not going in," he said. "I'm going to stay outside and keep my eyes open, anyhow."

I thought when I first went in that Victoria was alone in the room. Certainly Judy was nowhere about. I didn't know what had become of her. Just as Victoria spoke I saw Applebury standing in the big bay window gazing moodily out.

"Well, what have you got to tell us?"

Victoria's voice was jerky with frayed nerves and I didn't really hold her to account for her bad manners. But they produced a certain responsive stiffness in my own.

"I don't know anything about the robbery," I answered, "beyond the bare fact that Alec gave me over the telephone."

"Where's Judy?" she asked. "Do you know that?"

"Yes," I said. "She's here. She brought me up to the house. I expected to find her in this room."

"Is she married?" Victoria asked.

"Not yet," I said.

It wasn't until then that Applebury turned around and looked at me. I got the impression that my answer had startled him.

"I take it my cousin didn't come back with her," he said. "You don't know where he is, too, do you?"

"Not precisely," I said. "I believe he's out hunting an early rising parson to marry him to Judy."

"Why hasn't he got Judy with him then?" Victoria asked. "And why did she come back here with you?"

"I think I'd rather let Judy answer those questions," I told her. "I've come to see if I can be of any help about recovering the necklace."

"Your best assistance in that respect," said Applebury, "would lie in telling us, if you can, where and how we can get in communication with our departed guest."

"I don't think there'll be any difficulty about that," I said. "But I'd like to be told first what happened last night."

I realized that he was so angry that he could scarcely speak. He turned away from me now with a gesture of hardly repressed fury and left the answer I asked for to Victoria. She took it up.

"Bruce went to bed last night with the necklace under his pillow. We thought it would be safest in his care provided nobody knew he had it. No one was supposed to know it but Judy and me.

"Apparently she told Bruce's cousin, because Bruce was waked up some time in the middle of the night, by a little noise, probably, and saw there was a man in his room standing in front of his bureau by the head of his bed. A man in pajamas. Bruce spoke to him, and it turned out to be William Grant.

"He said he couldn't sleep and was out of cigarettes and had come in to get some. Bruce said there were some on the bureau, and told him to make a light so that he could see. His cousin said, 'No, I've found them, thanks,' and went back to his own room.

"That was all there was to it. Bruce went back to sleep and waked up before half past six. He felt under his pillow and found the necklace was gone. He looked in his cousin's room and found that he was gone too. He went out into the billiard room and saw that Alec's door was open, so he went in and told him about it. Alec came straight to me and I had him telephone to you."

So that was the way they meant to tell the story, was it, with Judy's note left out? Well, if they meant to fence with me, I'd fence with them.

"Have you any idea," I asked Applebury, "that Bill came into your room for any other purpose than to get the cigarettes?"

He turned upon me with an angry grin.

"It seems fairly obvious, doesn't it," he retorted, "that he came to get the necklace?"

"It doesn't seem obvious to me," I said. "Indeed, I find it hard to believe that you're making a charge like that seriously."

"He'll find that it's serious," Bruce predicted. "And I think you'll find that most people regard the inference as obvious."

"Not if we succeed in finding the real thief."

"Since you're so sure young Grant is innocent," Victoria put in, "I should think you'd be willing to tell us your version of his performance last night."

"I'm perfectly willing to do that," I answered.

It was declared war now between Victoria and me plainly enough. I couldn't have been neutral if I'd wanted to. So I went the whole hog.

"He eloped with Judy, and they came straight to my house. They told me they meant to be married as early this morning as possible. I agreed, after I'd heard the circumstances, that it was the thing for them to do, and offered my house for them to be married in. Bill went off to get his license and his parson, and Judy waited with me for him to come back with them. It was while we were waiting that Alec telephoned." I stopped for a long breath and then went on.

"My proposal to her was that she wait at my house and marry Bill, according to plan, when he came back. She refused to do that for reasons which I won't undertake to explain, left a note for Bill, and came back with me.

"I promise you there will be no difficulty about finding him. He'll come back to my house and then he'll follow on here. When he appears here is only a question of how long it takes him to get his license and to find his parson. In the meantime I suggest that we set about trying to find the person who stole the necklace."

Victoria's only comment was, "You've always hated me, haven't you?"

The barest possible denial was the only answer that I had to make to that. Bruce had more to say.

"Of course," he remarked, "if Mrs. Corbin wishes to go through the motions of searching for the necklace, there's no reason why she shouldn't. But it won't be found till my cousin, at some time that suits his convenience, produces it."

"Apparently," I observed, "you're not one of his friends."

His dark face flushed a little darker.

"I've never pretended to like him," he said. "But he's the nearest relation I've got, and I wanted to be on terms with him if possible. It has seemed more possible lately. I had the idea that he was settling down. That was my mistake. He's always been an anarchist; done what he liked, had what he wanted. He's never been under any decent discipline. This performance of his is like him enough, though it goes far beyond, of course, anything I've known him to do before."

"Which performance do you refer to?" I asked. "His eloping with Judy or his supposed theft of the necklace?"

"Both," he said.

"Let me be sure that I understand you. Do you think he pretended he wanted to marry Judy in order to steal the necklace? Or that he had meant to marry her and on the spur of the moment took the necklace instead? In either case I assume that you're not expecting him to come back."

He hesitated, then said, "I don't see why he shouldn't come back. In fact, I dare say he will. He'd see no reason why he shouldn't have Judy and the necklace as well. He's had plenty of time to hide it somewhere. He can come back now and submit to a search with all the innocence in the world. He can marry Judy and be safe. Don't you see the beauty of it? Once he's married to Judy, he's committed no crime at all. It's her necklace, and he's her husband. He figured that out, no doubt, before he came into my room."

"I take your point," I said, "but I shouldn't call it beautiful."

I was almost too angry to speak. Later I was to experience a certain feeling of sympathy for Bruce Applebury, but I wasn't aware of it then.

"Victoria," I said, "you certainly know Judy better than to accept any such monstrous theory as this. Judy and I know that Bill Grant isn't a thief. She's come back here because she wants the thief found. It's a point of honor with her that he shall be found. Won't you put matters in Alec's hands and start a search?"

I don't know what she'd have answered, for there was a knock on the door just then, and Punch came in. He was a desolate, pitiful little figure, white-faced, big-eyed, desperately serious.

"Grandmother sent me," he said. "She wants you to come into her room."

"How does *she* happen to be in on this?" Victoria demanded wildly. "Punch, have you been telling her about it?"

He confronted her panicky anger very steadily. He was much more adult in that moment than she.

"She called me in and asked me what had happened," he said. "She'd heard people moving about and Uncle Alec talking to me in the hall. I told her the necklace had been stolen again. From Bruce. She told me to go and send Judy to her, and I wouldn't because I knew Judy wasn't there and I didn't want Gran to know that she'd gone. But she made Digs wheel her into Judy's room. She saw Judy wasn't there, and then she came back. Just after that I saw Judy coming in, so I told her to go in and see Gran. I waited outside the door, and after a while Judy came and said Gran wanted to see you and Bruce."

"I'm glad she's found out about it," Bruce said. "Now perhaps we can get somewhere."

Victoria gave him a baleful look. I think at that moment she hated everybody in the world. There was nothing to be said, though. That summons could not be disregarded.

From the door she threw back a look at me. "You may as well come along too," she said.

It wasn't a very cordial or even courteous invitation but I made it serve.

Punch hung back to help me.

"You were a true prophet, Punch," I said. "You predicted big trouble, and here it is."

"I didn't think it would be as bad as this," he admitted.

"You look as if you'd had a night of it," I commented. "How did you know Judy had gone?"

"She had the necklace, you see," he said, "so I was keeping watch on the davenport the way I did the night before. And I saw her go out, her and Bill. They didn't know I saw them. So then I waited to see if they wouldn't come back. I was afraid I might go to sleep, so I walked up and down the hall here most of the time after they went. I'm glad she has come back," he added. "I knew she would."

Alec was patrolling the hall now, and he joined us.

"Did you get anywhere with Victoria?" he asked.

I shook my head. Then we both turned to see who was coming down from the floor above.

It was old Mr. Smith. He was dressed as carefully as if it had been ten o'clock in the morning, and he looked as if he hadn't a care in the world. I don't suppose he had, really. He was too old, too detached. He could be intensely interested in our plight without experiencing any painful emotions whatever over it.

"I understand the necklace has been stolen," he said as he came up. "How about it, Punch? Have you seen anything more of your man in pajamas?"

"No," Punch told him mournfully.

"What's that about a man in pajamas?" Alec demanded.

"It appears to be a private ghost of Punch's," old Eagle-Eye answered easily. "It walks when things are happening to the necklace."

"Well, I saw a man in pajamas last night," Alec said, a little embarrassed. He wasn't quite sure whether old Mr. Smith was joking or not.

But the old man turned that penetrating beam of his upon him and asked him crisply:

"Where did you see him? And when, if you know?"

"I haven't an idea when," said Alec. "I saw him come out of the bathroom in the Club."

"What sort of pajamas did he have on?"

"Oh, ordinary pajamas."

"You didn't notice whether there was a tear in them; one of those three-cornered tears, as if they'd been caught on a nail?"

"No," said Alec. "I didn't notice them at all. I didn't notice him at all. Why should I? He was just one of the guests coming out of the bathroom in the middle of the night and going back to his own room. There wasn't light enough to recognize him by and it didn't occur to me to try to. I was in my room with the door open. Naturally I didn't come out to see which door he turned into."

We had come to a halt just outside Mrs. Corbin's door.

"We mustn't keep Madame waiting," Mr. Smith said. And then he asked Alec, "Are you coming in to join the council of war?"

"No," Alec told him impatiently, "I think not. There has been too much consulting about this business, and I shan't be needed in there. I'd rather stay outside so that I can have some idea of what's going on in the house."

"I think you're quite right," said Mr. Smith, and he reached out and patted him approvingly—or so, at least, I interpreted the gesture at first—not quite on the chest, a little around to the left. Evidently his intelligent fingers found something, for he again expressed approval. "Good!" he said. "I've got one of them on, myself."

Then he knocked on Mrs. Corbin's door, and at her summons we both went in.

CHAPTER XVI

THE GENTLE ART

It was a big, dim, carpeted room, with long windows hung with heavy curtains and lambrequins. Excessive light and noise were carefully guarded against. There was a brown marble mantle, and all the tables, big and little, had brown marble tops.

The old lady, in her wheel chair, sat at the far end of the room, facing us as we came in. Judy—my first glance around had been to make sure she was there—sat drooping a little, but in an unusually formal attitude for her, on the couch in the corner. Bruce was in another corner sitting—evidently by command, and not liking it; one could see he'd rather have been on his feet—bolt upright on a hard little chair. Victoria, trying to look at ease and not succeeding very well at it, had seated herself near one of the windows.

The old lady greeted me with ceremonious courtesy, thanked me for having come, and directed Miss Digby to place a chair for me. Her greeting to old Mr. Smith was less formal.

"I thought I might need you as an expert, Ethelbert," she said. "But I doubt now if I shall."

Then she told Miss Digby she could go and waited in dead silence until the door was closed behind her.

Sad and humiliating as old Mrs. Corbin's bad periods must be—those times when, as Judy said, she was not presentable—it was already evident to me that at this particular early morning hour of this particular day she was as good as ever. I felt my spirits rising a little as this realization came home. Somehow I was counting another addition to Judy's phalanx. I don't know why I felt that the old matriarch would be on her side. There was nothing in Judy's forlorn appearance to warrant such a conclusion.

She opened with heavy artillery upon her daughter-in-law.

"It seems to me, Victoria,"—her voice crackled like sparks out of a coil—"that I have allowed you to make a mess of this business about long enough. I'm going to see what I can do with it myself."

"I haven't regarded the mess as of my making," Victoria retorted coolly enough—a little too coolly not to betray the fact that she was frightened.

She's always been afraid of old Mrs. Corbin. "However, I'll be glad to see what you make of it."

"Punch tells me ..." the old woman began again, and looked around as if in search of him. "I wanted him in here," she threw in, "but it doesn't matter. Punch tells me that the necklace has been stolen again."

Victoria nodded.

"It was taken last night, from Bruce ..." she began.

The old woman interrupted her. "I asked if it had been stolen, and you say it was. That's enough for the present. If it was stolen last night, I'd like to know what this is."

She stretched out a hand which had been lying in her lap and opened it. I jumped, and I think most of us did, for there dangled the necklace. Well, wait a minute;—a necklace, anyhow.

"I found it," she went on, "in Judy's room this morning. Judy herself wasn't there. She was running away, I understand, with her new young man. But she'd left this behind her, lying among the litter on her dressing table like a string of glass beads. I assume it's not the necklace that was stolen, but Ethelbert here will tell us, no doubt, whether it is or not, if you care to refer it to him."

"No," Victoria said dully. "It's an imitation I had made a little more than a year ago." She added with a spurt of anger, "You knew that all right, didn't you? I suppose Judy's been telling you all about it."

"Let Judy alone!" the old woman rapped out. "She's told me no secrets that weren't her own."

She turned from Victoria and addressed herself to Bruce Applebury, abandoning as she did so a good deal of her harshness of manner. Indeed for her she spoke almost gently. I scented danger for him, but apparently he did not.

"Judy tells me," Mrs. Corbin said, "that when she ran away with your cousin last night she meant to marry him. She says she'll marry him now if the necklace can be recovered, but that if it can not be recovered, she stands ready to marry you. A wedding is a bargain, and it takes two to make it. Are you still willing to marry her?"

"Yes," Bruce said. "Certainly. That's all I ask; to go on as if nothing had happened."

He glanced toward Judy, but she gave no sign of having heard him or of even knowing that he was in the room.

"She understands that, I think," he went on a little less confidently. "We talked it out pretty thoroughly yesterday afternoon."

"The necklace hadn't been stolen then," the old lady remarked. "Where was it?"

"It happened to be in my pocket," Bruce said. "I'd gone into town to get it and she met me at the train."

"Whose was it then?" Mrs. Corbin asked him.

The question obviously took him aback and he repeated it stupidly. She flung it back at him. "Yes, to whom did the necklace belong then?"

"I understood," he said, "that it belonged to you."

"You're perfectly right," she assured him grimly. "It did. And last night at dinner I gave it to Judy. It was my intention, at least, to give it to her, and give it I did, although it wasn't the thing she put around her neck. The real necklace was hers last night. But whose was it when it was stolen, Mr. Applebury?"

He perceived the pitfall now, but too late to keep from plunging into it. He was neither a naturally endowed nor a practised liar.

"Why—it was hers, I suppose," he said.

"Hadn't she given it to you?"

He flushed deeply. "I hadn't accepted it," he said.

"Do you believe your cousin stole it?" she asked.

"That's not a pleasant conclusion to come to," he told her. "But it's hard to see how one can believe anything else."

"Don't palaver," the old woman snapped at him. "Do you believe he stole it?"

Bruce hesitated, looking acutely unhappy, but at last he said, "Yes, I do."

"Judy doesn't," Mrs. Corbin returned. "She says she'd marry him now if the necklace could be recovered. She wouldn't marry anyone she believed to be a thief. But she seems to feel that you have a right either to her or to the necklace. If she can't produce the necklace, she's bound to marry you. Is that the way you look at it yourself?"

"That's a perfectly unfair way of putting it," he protested.

She gave a short grim laugh.

"It'll serve well enough I think," she said.

In the next breath she pounced upon him again.

"Victoria had pawned the necklace, of course. Did you redeem it for her?"

"Yes," he admitted sulkily, "I did."

"How much did it cost you?" she asked.

He told her, "Twenty-five thousand dollars."

"That was very handsome of you," she observed, not satirically, but quite as if she meant it.

He started to tell her he'd been glad to do it, but before the words were half uttered, she'd turned to Victoria.

"Did you tell Judy," she asked, "that you had come down on her fiancé for the money?"

"No," Victoria answered, "of course not."

The gathering cloud of the old woman's anger was a positively appalling thing to watch.

"Then," she said at last, turning back to Bruce, "you must have told her yourself."

You couldn't deny the possession of a certain stiff sort of courage to that young man. He stood up to her.

"Yes," he said, "I told her. She'd met me at the train with the information that she'd planned to jilt me for that worthless cousin of mine. I'd engaged myself in good faith to marry her. I'd come out here with my friends and my family to do it. And then, here on the day before the wedding, she wanted to cry off.

"I'd advanced a substantial sum of money to her mother on the supposition that the wedding was to take place. I thought it was only fair she should know it. She took the same view of it that I did, and agreed to marry me. I didn't suggest—it would have been unthinkable, of course—that I take the necklace as an alternative."

"The necklace wasn't hers at that time to offer as an alternative," Mrs. Corbin pointed out. "I hadn't given it to her then. When I did, she gave it to you—by word of mouth, or did she put it in writing?"

"She left a note last night," Bruce told her, "in which she said that I might keep the pearls. But apparently my cousin didn't agree to that disposal of them."

"And, that being the case, you're willing to marry my granddaughter?"

The biting irony in her voice could not be ignored, but he answered stiffly, "Yes, I am. But I think your insinuation is outrageously unfair. You seem to be trying to make it appear that I'm to blame for all this. I've come out here to keep my part of a bargain, and all I'm asking, as a matter of simple justice, is that your granddaughter shall keep hers. I haven't deceived anybody nor lied to anybody, nor tried to take unfair advantage of anybody. It seems to me that the shoe is on the other foot."

"You needn't worry about simple justice," said the old woman grimly. "You're going to get it. When you told that child that you'd redeemed the necklace for her mother you practically told her you'd bought her. But I'm not willing to let her go at that price. She's worth more than you paid, just as the necklace is. You shall have your money back as soon as I can write you a check."

There's no doubt at all that Bruce felt himself abominably ill used. He hadn't transgressed his own code in telling Judy the obligation her mother had saddled her with. He considered, no doubt, that he was acting magnanimously in forgetting, so to speak, Judy's adventure with Bill. He must, of course, have been passionately desirous of her or he wouldn't have done that. But there was a hotter fuel for his anger than all this came to, I think.

This was the knowledge that in another particular he had transgressed his code. It was his hatred of his cousin that had betrayed him into it. One can imagine that this hatred must have been latent for years. He'd spoken of him to me that morning as an undisciplined anarchist who had done what he liked, had what he wanted. The care-free grasshopper—don't you see?—viewed by the laborious ant and never overtaken by the winter.

His discovery, early that morning, that Bill had taken Judy away from him had driven him to an act that demolished his own self-righteousness. As I said before, I really pitied him when I understood. That wasn't my feeling at the present moment, though.

His face had gone livid with anger under the lash of the old woman's last words. He sprang to his feet.

"Very well," he said. "I can't dispute your right to discharge the obligation in that way. But that's not going to be the end of it. If your granddaughter wants to marry my cousin, she'll have to marry a proclaimed thief. He may never be sent to jail for what he's done. That decision's in your hands too, I suppose. But the story of it shall follow him as long as he lives."

There was a furious retort on the old woman's lips, but it was checked by the quiet tones of old Mr. Smith.

"Augusta," he said (I'd never heard her addressed by that name before, and it made me jump), "have I your permission to take a hand?"

She nodded without a word, and sank back with a sigh into her chair.

Old Eagle~Eye turned to Bruce.

"Please sit down again," he said persuasively. "I don't think we need be violent about this. The suggestion I wish to make is that you make a beginning at once and tell us the story now. I've heard no account of the robbery myself, and I don't think Mrs. Corbin has. If there really is a clear case against your cousin, we'd like to hear it."

Disarming as his voice was, I don't know that Applebury would have yielded if the old man hadn't added, "Of course you'd want to tell it, at least for once, in the presence of any of us who might have contributory testimony of our own to offer."

"I'm not afraid of any contributory testimony," Bruce said. "Yes, I'll be glad to tell it."

I felt, as he went ahead and detailed in a painstakingly literal manner, without comment and without betrayal of passion, the incident which Victoria had related to me a little earlier, that it made at best a terribly damaging story. It seemed to me just as it seemed to Judy that it was refutable only by the discovery of the actual thief. Not even Bill's return—lord, how I wished he would come, though—could clear him of the shabby crime Bruce was charging him with.

Even old Mr. Smith betrayed, as he listened, the nearest approach to excitement he was capable of. His manner was calm enough, but his eye had the old irrepressible eagle gleam in it. It seemed to me that Bruce had gone as fully as possible into details, but there hadn't been enough of these to satisfy the old gentleman. He took Applebury back over the story from the beginning.

"You'd gone to bed somewhere about two o'clock, wasn't it, with the necklace under your pillow, and fallen asleep? Did that happen at once or did you have any trouble getting off?"

"I lay awake a while," Bruce said. "I don't know how long."

"Everything was quiet then, was it? Bill hadn't kept you awake by moving about?"

"No, it was quiet. I think he got to bed before I did."

"And there was no light in his room?"

"I didn't see any."

"So you had no reason to think that he wasn't out of the way until morning," Mr. Smith commented.

Bruce didn't dissent to that.

"Well, then," the old man went on, "you fell asleep. Deeply?"

"I'm a fairly sound sleeper," said Bruce.

"And you didn't waken till Bill came into the room?"

"I think not. No, I'm sure I didn't."

"Do you know what waked you up?"

"I haven't an idea—some noise, I suppose. I don't know that it was that. It may have been some movement about my bed."

"Such as a hand under your pillow?" suggested Mr. Smith.

"It may have been that," Bruce agreed grimly. "As I say, I don't know. I found myself awake."

"You don't think Bill had spoken to you from his room before he came in?"

"I'm very sure," said Bruce, "that he did not. He was standing there, in his pajamas, close by the head of my bed, rummaging over the top of my bureau."

"He'd left a light on in his room, I suppose," Mr. Smith suggested, "and the door was open behind him?"

"I don't know about the door," said Bruce. "There was no light coming in from his room. There was no light at all except what came in from outdoors."

"You didn't instantly recognize him, then?"

"Naturally not. I asked who it was."

"And he replied that it was Bill and that he'd come in for some cigarettes?"

Bruce nodded. He seemed to be getting bored with all these repetitions.

"And you suggested that he turn on the light?"

"We've been over all that," Bruce said impatiently. "Yes."

"His voice sounded perfectly natural and matter-of-fact?"

"I suppose so," Bruce admitted. "Yes, I can't say that it didn't."

"So you had no impression whatever of anything furtive or stealthy about his way of coming in?"

"I don't think I'd say that," Bruce objected. "I think it *was* rather stealthy. I know that it struck me at the time as rather queer that I hadn't heard him coming in."

"You are sure you were perfectly broad awake when you did see him there?" Mr. Smith asked.

"Yes, I'm sure of that. I think my asking him why he didn't turn on the light shows it."

The old man nodded gravely. "Yes," he said. "I think we may regard that as conclusive."

I got a sort of thrill out of that, and looking over at Judy I saw she'd got it too. But I didn't, even then, know what he was driving at.

He went on in a somewhat thoughtful tone.

"So he took his cigarettes and went away, closing his door after him, I think you said. And you once more dropped off to sleep. And that's the story."

He sat in thoughtful silence over it for a moment.

Then he looked straight at Bruce and asked, "Mr. Applebury, was the necklace under your pillow at that time?"

Bruce returned his gaze with a frightened stare.

"In the light of what I've found out since," he said, when he could make his voice come, "I think it's natural to assume that it was not."

"I asked," said Mr. Smith, and now his voice was like a shining sword, "I asked for your personal knowledge. Was the necklace under your pillow when your cousin went back to his room?"

"I don't know," Bruce said. "It was gone in the morning anyhow."

"We'll come to the morning presently. Mr. Applebury, let me ask you to consider what you've told us.

"You'd gone to bed guarding a priceless thing which was in some danger of being stolen. You had chosen to guard it by putting it under your pillow, where by a touch, by the smallest movement of your hand, you could assure yourself from time to time of its safety. You were startled out of a deep sleep by the presence of an unknown man in your room, a man whose entrance, by your own statement, had seemed stealthy and unexplained. You didn't know who he was until he spoke in answer to your question.

"Do you pretend to assert seriously that your hand never moved under the pillow to discover whether the necklace was still there?"

Bruce sprang to his feet.

"Look here," he said, through colorless lips, "I've been insulted far enough."

"Sit down," commanded old Eagle-Eye. "I'm going to insult you a little further. You've made a statement which the mind of a child would reject as preposterous. I make the counter-statement that you did feel under the pillow; that you knew that the necklace was there before your cousin had had time to tell you who he was; that unless it had been there you would have raised an outcry upon the spot. You dropped asleep contentedly after he had gone back to his room because you knew it was still there."

There was a moment of dead silence. Bruce didn't even try to speak. I felt, after the first flush of crude triumph, something painfully humiliating in the spectacle of as complete a demolition as that, even of one I'd been regarding as an enemy.

Judy felt it too. She sprang up and ran to the window where she stood looking out. I could see the tears running down her face—partly from relief, of course, over the clearing of her lover, but partly, I think, from pity. She had no disposition to gloat over him, anyhow.

Mr. Smith was the only one of us who remained unmoved. He hadn't completely finished.

"Now we'll come to the events of this morning. I don't know, Mr. Applebury, where the necklace was when you wakened. It may have been taken by a thief after you had dropped asleep again. Or it may have still been under your pillow."

Bruce had found his voice again. "Do you mean to insinuate ..." he began.

"Not at this moment," interrupted Mr. Smith. "I'll do my insinuating a little later.

"As I said, we don't know where the necklace was when you waked up this morning. But we do know that upon your bureau, left there by your cousin, Bill Grant, was a note from Judy telling you that you might keep the necklace, and that at that price she was quit of you.

"We know that his actual errand to your room was to leave that note; that it was for this purpose that he had undressed and gone to bed and waited for you to fall asleep.

"We know with what feelings you regard your cousin. It doesn't want much imagination to picture you as furiously angry, as anxious to avenge the humiliation you felt he had put upon you. The fact that your cousin had been in the room during the night and that he had now left his room and the house, offered you an apparently easy revenge.

"Now I'll make my insinuation, if you like. We have nothing but your unsupported assertion that any robbery whatever has taken place. You lied in accusing your cousin of the theft, and I find it easy to believe that you have lied in declaring that any theft occurred."

CHAPTER XVII

SOME MUST WATCH

I looked at Bruce in astonishment. In everything but the bare form of the words he had been accused of having, himself, stolen the necklace, and it was amazing the way the accusation had brought him back to life again. His moment of collapse was past. His face was afire with anger. He turned upon me.

"I decline to rest under this infamous charge," he said. "I insist upon being searched at once; that my room and my effects be searched. That necklace was gone when I waked up this morning."

He turned upon Mr. Smith. "You can't accuse an honest man of theft and get away with it."

"I'm glad you've made that discovery," the old gentleman replied quietly. "However, I haven't made a charge. Nothing but the same sort of insinuation which you made against your cousin. The necklace may have been stolen after he and Judy left the house last night. I'm inclined to think it was."

"Have we got to go on *talking*?" Bruce demanded of me. "Can't we go in my room and begin the search?"

It was rather pathetic, his turning to me like that. Relatively, I suppose, I seemed like a friend. It's a fact that I was sorry for him and that I believed he knew no more of the present whereabouts of the necklace than I did.

Old Eagle-Eye was in charge, however, and I referred to him for his consent. He gave it by rising, with a bow to old Mrs. Corbin.

"I think we'd better adjourn up-stairs," he said. "That's the real field of battle anyhow."

"You'll come too, sir, won't you?" Bruce asked me. And when I agreed, he handed me my crutches and helped me to my feet.

"I've never been searched before," he remarked gloomily as we rode up in the elevator together. "I've never even seen a man searched."

"I never have either," I confessed nervously. I think I dreaded the ordeal almost as much as he. There is something rather horrifying about the idea.

But we might have spared our apprehensions, for the search, as it happened, never came off.

The elevator shaft on the top floor opens directly into the billiard room. Bruce opened the door when the car stopped and stepped out, but since there was a slight inequality between levels, he turned back instantly to caution me about it. I swung myself out without difficulty, but I all but lost my balance and fell back into the car from sheer astonishment at what I saw.

"Good lord!" I gasped. "Punch, what in the world are you doing?"

Mr. Smith was at my side in an instant, and his right hand went under his coat, even before he saw what I was looking at.

The little boy never turned his head. He was standing beside the billiard table, covering with his trusty rifle one of the closed doors down at the end of the room. He was still very pale, but his eyes were shining now, and his hands were steady.

"Look out," he said quietly. "He's in the trunk closet."

"Who is?" Bruce demanded. "What do you mean?"

But Mr. Smith asked no questions. He whipped out the automatic pistol from under his coat.

"It's all right if you're sure he's there," he said. "I've got the door covered too."

"Well, I'm pretty sure," said Punch. "I saw a drop of oil on the hinge. That's how I know."

"Any other way out of it than through that door?" Mr. Smith asked briskly, but speaking low as the boy had done.

"No," said Punch. "It's an awfully big place. It goes clear around the corner. But that's the only way out, unless he's made a hole in the roof."

"They're slate shingles," Mr. Smith observed. "He's still in there, then."

"What are they talking about?" Bruce demanded of me.

"The thief's in there," Mr. Smith told him. "Punch's ghost, the man in pajamas. Look here, can you shoot quick and straight if you have to? If you can I'll give you this pistol. I'm going to open the door."

He held the weapon out to Bruce. "With my apologies," he added.

"Thanks very much, sir," said Bruce. "But I'll open the door myself."

Mr. Smith nodded.

"Stand to one side when you do," he cautioned him. "Don't get in our line of fire."

"If he's the man who stole the necklace," Bruce remarked, "you won't have to shoot. Not if I can get my hands on him."

I don't very much mind admitting that my own emotions combined a lively curiosity about that door whose oiled hinges had indicated it as the robber's hiding-place, with an intense desire to get back into the elevator. Try participating in a scene like that upon a pair of crutches before you allow yourself to feel too contemptuous over this admission.

Bruce had already started for the door, but he couldn't go in a straight line to it because of the corner of the billiard table. Before he could get around this obstruction a new voice spoke and halted him in his tracks.

"Really there's no need for any sort of violence," it stated, irritably. "I'll open the door myself. I'll hold my hands out before me and you'll see that it won't be necessary to shoot. That's quite understood, is it?"

"Perfectly," Mr. Smith agreed. "We won't do anything impulsive. Open the door."

The door swung open noiselessly, and there, true to his promise, stood a man holding out a pair of empty hands.

His appearance is rather hard to describe, since the obvious facts about it seemed fortuitous and somehow contradictory to the truer ones. He was, for example, unmistakably dirty and disheveled. Yet he looked as if he ought to be scrupulously clean and tidy. You felt that it was contradictory to his nature to go more than twenty-four hours without a shave, although a shadow of colorless beard upon his plump cheeks proclaimed that he had done so. He was plump, although he happened just now to be rather haggard and hungry-looking. His suit of clothes was cheap and shapeless, yet something about him proclaimed him a fop. His grimy hands were small and finely formed, and as fastidious as Mr. Smith's.

His glance shifted swiftly from one to another of us, coming to rest at last in sour contemplation upon Punch.

The boy had been gazing at him intently, groping for an identification. Now he got it.

"Why," he cried, "he's the man who was hanging the new window shades. He must have been in there ever since Wednesday."

That afforded me a grin. I turned to Mr. Smith. "That's been Punch's theory from the beginning, you know," I remarked. "He discussed with me Wednesday morning the danger that one of the artisans about the place would conceal himself in the house and steal the necklace when he got a chance. He spent most of that day and the next patroling the house, trying to guard against that very thing happening."

"Good for Punch," said Mr. Smith, but in so preoccupied a tone that it fell far short of the handsome acknowledgment I wanted for the boy's cleverness.

I persisted, speaking now to Punch. "I wonder if you were right about the actual moment when the imitation necklace was taken?"

Without pausing I put the thing up to the burglar. "Was it Thursday afternoon about two o'clock, just before the guests got here, that you made your raid on Mrs. Corbin's safe?"

The man didn't answer. But to put it this way doesn't at all describe what happened. It was utterly preposterous. This trapped little rat of a thief, haggard, grimy, unshaved, tried to make me feel—and almost, I swear, succeeded—as if I'd just spoken to a duke to whom I'd not been properly introduced. He did it with a perfectly impassive face and an almost imperceptible turning of the shoulders.

But at that, old Mr. Smith got what he'd been looking for.

"Raglan, by George!" he exclaimed. "This is a real pleasure. But man, I'd hardly have known you!"

The thief showed no reciprocal delight in the recognition. Indeed his look of disgust deepened. But he spoke for the first time since he'd opened the door.

"Really," he said, "I should hope not. I've been living in that filthy box room three days, feeding on a particularly nasty sort of American milk chocolate. I haven't been able to shave since Thursday night."

He spoke with a marked British accent, which didn't, however, satisfy my ear. It was just about as good an imitation, I decided, as Victoria's Japanese pearls.

"Horribly unpleasant, I should think," Mr. Smith agreed sympathetically.

Then he explained to the rest of us. "Mr. Raglan is not only one of the most expert gem thieves in the world; he's also admitted to be the best dressed man in his profession."

Bruce Applebury wasn't in a sympathetic mood. He made no acknowledgment whatever of the honor of the introduction to so eminent a craftsman. He said to Mr. Smith, "We must call the police at once, of course. Shall I telephone?"

"Oh, there's no hurry, I think," said Mr. Smith. "It's still frightfully early."

He turned to the thief. "Raglan," he said, "I'm going to propose a bargain. You produce the necklace; save us the trouble of a search for it. If you'll do that, I'll take the liberty of promising you, although I'm merely one of Mrs. Corbin's guests, a bath and a shave, a change of linen, and a really good breakfast. All that before presenting you to the police—and the photographers."

"Done," said Raglan, without a moment's hesitation. "Thanks very much."

He slid his right hand under his coat toward his left armpit.

"Look out!" Bruce cried sharply. "He's after a gun."

Raglan's answer was to unbutton his coat and throw it back, showing that there was no weapon there.

But Mr. Smith had betrayed no perturbation, even before he got this reassurance. "Unless Raglan has changed his well-known methods," he said, "he doesn't carry a gun. He has a strong aversion to the more unpleasant forms of violence. He has compromised with necessity to the length of a delicately wielded blackjack, and you'll probably find that his equipment includes a small bottle of chloroform. But it's not on record that he's ever killed anyone."

Raglan made no comment upon these remarks. He was busy with the lining of his sleeve, just beneath the armpit. He had, it appeared, a long pocket in there. Presently he pulled out the necklace.

Here and now, I make my apologies for the banal philosophizings I had addressed, at lunch time on the previous day, to its substitute. It was worth all the labor it had cost. It was above price—a masterpiece. The glory of it held the five of us spellbound, the connoisseur, the disappointed thief, the lover who had tried to include it in his bargain, the small boy and myself. We didn't speak; we hardly breathed. I think Raglan might have bolted had he not been bound by the same enchantment as the rest of us.

At last old Mr. Smith broke the spell.

"Punch," he said, "take this down-stairs and give it to your grandmother. Tell her that none of her guests nor of her family had anything to do with its disappearance. Nor her servants either. Ask her if she's willing that Belden should send up a good hearty breakfast to an old acquaintance of mine whom I am entertaining in my room."

Punch's hands were shaking as Mr. Smith gently deposited the treasure in the cup he made of them. I remembered the negligence with which the imitation had been reconsigned to the boy's old pocket handkerchief the day before and wondered that I had not guessed the truth from that.

"I'm to tell Gran nothing but that?" Punch asked, his eyes dancing with excitement. "And I'm not to tell anyone else anything at all?"

"Not if you can help it," said old Eagle-Eye with a grin. "We must keep our bargain with Raglan if we can. Go on and find Belden, if your grandmother gives you leave, and order the breakfast from him. Then come back here."

Punch darted off on his errand.

I think perhaps the return of the necklace to Mrs. Corbin served to remind Bruce of his own injuries and disappointments. It was with a very sulky expression that he watched the boy disappear down the stairs.

"I really can't understand," he said, turning impatiently back to Mr. Smith, "why a professional criminal should be treated with such extraordinary consideration. He ought to be in handcuffs now and on his way to jail."

"Surely you can understand keeping a bargain," Mr. Smith answered suavely. "I've heard you discourse feelingly on that subject within the hour."

Applebury's only reply to that was an angry shrug of the shoulders. I think he suspected the old gentleman of meaning to let the thief go altogether now that the necklace was recovered.

I didn't go as far as that, but I was a little uneasy lest his zest in the new game he was playing—I hadn't yet made out what it was—should betray the old gentleman into trusting too far to Mr. Raglan's dislike of violence.

"My room and bath are entirely at your disposal now, Mr. Raglan," he said, leading the way toward his door and opening it. "As to the change of linen I promised you, I'm afraid I'd been counting on Mr. Applebury's acquiescence in my bargain. My own perhaps can be made to serve."

Bruce's face on hearing the suggestion that he provide the burglar with a shirt and a suit of underclothes was a study in outraged astonishment. But he was prevented from further expressing his feelings by Raglan's answer. Raglan, it appeared, was equally affronted by the proposal.

"That won't be necessary," he said coldly. "I have a bag with me. Perhaps the young man will bring it out. I'd be glad to fetch it myself but I don't suppose that would quite meet your ideas. It's standing on the first box around the corner."

"Get it out, will you, Applebury?" said old Mr. Smith.

I really thought Bruce would burst. His neck distinctly swelled above his collar. But he marched off in high dudgeon toward the trunk closet, to return a moment later lugging a big black case of a nondescript sort. It was rather battered, and would have passed muster all right as the sort of thing a workman could carry tools in.

Bruce set it down without a word, and walked off to his own room. I have never seen him, I remark with thankfulness, since.

Raglan picked up the bag and followed Mr. Smith into his room, I swinging along after them on my crutches, feeling rather nervous over Bruce's defection. That little man might easily be too much, I thought, for Mr. Smith and me.

Raglan would have carried the bag straight on through into the bathroom if Mr. Smith hadn't halted him.

"I think perhaps," he said, "you'd better take off your clothes out here. Then you can bathe and shave in privacy, and we can wait your convenience."

I saw the point to that, as Raglan did, and felt a little better. There was a window in the bathroom, big enough for a man to climb out of, and there might be a handy down-spout that would take him to the ground. But no thief, no matter how desperate, would try to escape without his clothes.

Raglan, stripped to his underwear, opened the bag, lifted out a tray of tools, and selected his clean linen. Then he went into the bathroom and locked the door behind him.

"I suppose," I remarked, "he might have had that necklace hidden where we'd have had the devil's own time finding it."

"No, I hardly think so," Mr. Smith dissented politely. "No, that's not the reason I'm coddling him. He's dirty and miserable, and ravenously hungry,

I suspect. When he's clean and fed, he'll be expansive. I want him to tell me how he did it, and if they'll only let us alone for half an hour, I believe he will. Ah, here's Punch. Now we'll know."

CHAPTER XVIII

PEACOCK FEATHERS

As usual, Mr. Smith turned out to be right. You wouldn't have known Raglan for the same man when he came out of that bathroom, and the transformation was completed when he had arrayed himself with scrupulous care and deliberation in an exquisitely tailored light gray suit with a fine blue stripe in it, symphonically harmonious with his socks and his cravat, brushed his hair, and settled himself at the little table where his breakfast was arrayed. I wondered as I watched his delicate approach to the chilled grapefruit whether, had I seen him first like this, I should have detected anything imitative or unreal about his well~bred English accent.

Punch had been watching these proceedings with breathless interest.

"Are the pajamas in there?" he asked, indicating the tool box. "The ones with the tear in the leg?"

Raglan nodded, indifferently enough, and then rather suddenly arrested his spoon for a thoughtful look at the boy.

"Yes," he said, presently, turning back to his breakfast, "they're down at the bottom, with the window shade hanger's tools. Get them out, if you're interested. Keep them for a souvenir. I never want to see them again."

Punch had them out in a minute. There they were, sure enough. Lavender silk pajamas, with a big nail tear in one of the legs.

"They're really an important souvenir," Mr. Smith observed. "They must have been the main inspiration of the—campaign."

"Naturally," Raglan said. "There's no trick about getting into any house, nor about hiding in it. But how to stay hidden for as long as may be necessary—well, the pajamas struck me as a pretty good answer. I could lie up by day almost anywhere providing I had freedom to move about at night. In a big house like this, full of guests who weren't likely to know one another any too well, I'd be sure to have it. No one would pay any attention to a man in pajamas on his way to the bathroom. I could get all I needed to drink. I could shave, I thought, every night. I did shave, as a matter of fact, Wednesday night and Thursday night. It looked easy—a little too easy, I fancy. It was probably one of my mistakes. I've made several of them on this job, you know."

"We shall have to rely upon you to tell us what they were," said Mr. Smith politely. "The main conception was, it seems to me, quite in your best vein. Indeed I blame myself for failing to recognize your—idiom, so to speak, in the mere prima facie aspects of the case."

The fellow was vain as a peacock, I could see. He was drinking down the old man's compliments like wine. I ventured to lend a hand.

"You weren't very far from it," I reminded Mr. Smith. "The thing had a certain look to you which you kept reverting to, which made it hard for you to believe it to be the work of an amateur."

"I failed to think clear through to the edge," the old gentleman confessed mournfully. "I fell before the irresistible presumption which imposed on everyone else; the presumption that a man wandering about the house at night in bath-slippers and pajamas must be one of the guests. And that despite the clear clue we had to the contrary, in the failure of Punch's review of all the pajamas in the house that had been slept in, to account for the pair with a nail tear in the leg."

This time it was Raglan's coffee cup that halted sharply on the way to his lips.

"Punch!" he murmured, and turned another thoughtful look on the little boy.

But he was too hungry to be diverted more than momentarily from his breakfast, and Mr. Smith let him alone until he'd finished it. Then he offered him a cigar, and said, "I'd like to begin at the beginning. You came to the house ostensibly to put up window shades."

"Ostensibly!" Raglan put in. "I worked here for two days; I must have put up hundreds of them, all over the house—practically all over the house. I couldn't get into the old lady's room. There was no work of any sort being done there. But the rest of the house I came to know like the palm of my hand.

"Wednesday afternoon when the old woman went around in her wheelchair, attended by her grandson, assigning rooms to the people who were coming, I was working up on this floor and I learned the names of everyone who was coming and where everyone was to sleep, which helped a lot."

"And a little later that afternoon," Mr. Smith observed, "when it was time for the workmen to quit, instead of leaving the house you moved into the room you'd selected for yourself and made yourself at home. You know, I wonder a little at your choice of a hiding-place, the top floor of the house with only one flight of stairs leading to it and only one door out of the place, once you'd got in."

Raglan laughed—not a very nice sort of laugh, either.

"I thought of all that," he said. "But there were compensating advantages. I found them the first time I went in there. You can hear everything that's said in both sitting rooms, the old lady's and her daughter's—by some trick of construction that I didn't figure out."

"I know about that," Punch volunteered. "The light comes up too. I asked grandmother why it was once, and she said grandfather had had the tops left off the window casings so that the long windows would slide all the way up."

"I no longer wonder at your choice of it as a hiding place," Mr. Smith remarked dryly.

He took the staggering revelation, though, a good deal more calmly than I did. Heavens, how much did the man know! What was there that he didn't know! I began to understand the basis for the fellow's extraordinary complacency in confessing the details of his crime before three witnesses. Mr. Smith did nothing to disturb it.

"When was it you stole the imitation necklace from Mrs. Corbin's safe?" he asked. "Wednesday night?"

Raglan shook his head. "I hadn't a chance. I'd planned to, but the old woman wouldn't quiet down; kept ringing for her nurse, and quarreling with her; wanted more dope than the nurse would give her, evidently. So I had to wait. I got my chance the next day. Just the time the lad here thought. I don't know how he figured it out. The servants were all at lunch, I knew, and the family out on the veranda waiting for the guests to come. It was a close connection but I figured the safe wouldn't give me any trouble, and it didn't. I didn't waste any time about it though.

"I got the necklace, dropped it in my pocket, shut the safe and came out into the hall. Everything was all right and I had a clear out, down the servants' stairs. I had my case with me and anybody I might have met would have thought I'd come back that morning to finish up.

"I stood there with my hand in my pocket, feeling of the necklace. I hadn't taken time to examine it. It hadn't occurred to me to doubt that it was all right. But it did now. The feel of it was just a shade off, enough to make me suspicious.

"Just then I heard someone coming up the main stairs, so I went up instead of down. Back to that damned box room. There I turned my torch on the thing and saw at once that I'd been done. So I settled down to think it out.

"The old lady had been done, too, some time or other. That was plain enough. There was no doubt about her thinking this was the right string. There wasn't any doubt, either, when I thought it over, that by taking the phony string I'd played straight into somebody's hands. Whoever had made the substitution had nothing more to worry about now. I was the goat and I didn't like it.

"Of course, if the real necklace had actually been stolen and disposed of there was no help for it. But there was almost as good a chance that it had been borrowed—pawned perhaps.

"That seemed more likely the more I thought about it. Whoever had pawned it must have been sweating blood over what would happen when the old woman gave the necklace to the girl. They'd have one good laugh over the boob who'd stolen the imitation necklace, and think no more about it.

"Well, then, why not put the phony string back in the old woman's room? It might not do anything more than take the laugh off me. But it might, you see, do duty as a decoy for the real one. Besides, it would make everybody think that some fool amateur had taken the thing, lost his nerve and brought it back. Head off a lot of prying around.

"That night I started out in my pajamas, had a bath and shaved in the nearest bathroom, went downstairs and put the necklace back. I'd have put it back in the safe, but the nurse was sleeping there that night, so I didn't chance it. I went back upstairs feeling pretty good. And then I got a devil of a jolt."

Punch grinned. "When I came up-stairs after you," he asked, "and turned on the light in the billiard room?"

"My God!" murmured Raglan after a long stare at him.

"You see," said Punch, "I saw the pajamas going across in the moonlight. That's how I knew about the tear in the leg. There are lots of nails sticking out in the trunk closet. I might have thought of that. But when you went up-stairs I couldn't think why anybody should, or rather, why anybody who slept up-stairs should have come down, so I followed up to see. Well, I didn't see anything or hear anything, so I came back. I was sort of scared myself."

The first look of bewilderment in Raglan's face had deepened into one of sour disgust. Mr. Smith set about restoring his complacency.

"Well, your plan worked," he commented. "The imitation necklace served to decoy the real one back just as you meant it to.

"If you remember," he added, turning to me, "it was the curiously imaginative quality of this stroke which gave the whole affair to my mind the look—what you will perhaps allow me to call the style—we were speaking of. I should have recognized his handiwork from that alone."

Raglan beamed again and took a dainty draught or two of his cigar.

"Oh, there was nothing to it really," he said, with a falsely deprecatory air that made me want to hit him. "It needed a bit of luck to put it through, but I had it right enough, and I knew I had it too.

"I heard our young friend Applebury getting his instructions, the first thing yesterday morning, to go to the bank and get the real necklace. I knew it would be somewhere in this house before night.

"I didn't know where it would be. It might turn out to be in any one of four places. The girl might have it, or her mother, or her grandmother—though I doubted if they'd trust it again to that Noah's Ark of a safe.

"But it struck me that the best chance of all was Applebury. He'd put up his money for it, and he'd hang on to it if he could. So I decided to try his room first.

"I made another of my mistakes then. I didn't realize that there was anyone left alive in the world who'd be such a fool as to try to guard a thing by sleeping with it under his pillow. I thought he'd either hide it seriously, or else attach it somehow to his person; put it on around his neck. That would have been the simplest thing.

"I chose the other alternative first, since it wouldn't involve giving him a tap on the head. I began a search of the room. I began with the bureau, and found it wasn't there. Then I heard someone coming, and slid into the bay-window, behind one of the curtains. There was an amateur thief on the job it seemed, in pajamas just as I was.

"I watched him pretty close through a crack between the curtain and the wall. It was possible, of course, that he'd get the thing. He was a rank amateur all right. He hadn't rummaged more than a second or two over the bureau top before he hit something with his hand and moved it with a rattle.

"Applebury waked up, and I never wanted to laugh more, when I couldn't afford to, than I did then. Because he slid his hand straight under his pillow and showed me where the thing was. Then he said, 'Who's there?' Another fool thing to do. It was his cousin, Grant, as I suppose you know. Grant said he'd come in for cigarettes, took them, and went away.

"I stayed where I was of course, and waited for things to quiet down. They didn't for quite a while. Grant was ramming around in the next room, trying to dress without making a light. I was afraid he'd waken everybody on the floor. He didn't, though, and at last I heard him go down the stairs.

"But the house didn't quiet down perfectly even then. Every little while I'd hear a sound. Something was going on, and I couldn't make out what it was. Of course I stayed right where I was by the window. I hadn't stirred out of my tracks. I had stood there so long I felt as if I'd grown to the rug. Applebury was sound asleep again. No need waiting any longer for him.

"Then I happened to look out the window, and saw Grant and the girl making a get-away. Well, that was made to order for me, or so it looked anyhow. I might have known it looked too good to be true.

"It involved a change in my plan, of course. I had meant to shave and go back to the box room and wait till the time of the wedding this afternoon. I knew there'd be hundreds of people here, with a special train coming down from town and all that. Then I'd put on these clothes that I'm wearing now, come down-stairs, and be one of the guests. I even thought of staying for the ceremony and picking up a ride back to town.

"It was a pretty sort of idea, the sort that looks good when you think of it, although on general principles the sooner you can get away after you've got what you've come for, the better.

"Now, of course, there was no question about it. The girl had gone and there wouldn't be any wedding, and with the necklace gone, on top of that, there would be one hell of a commotion.

"The thing for me to do was to get out. There'd be no question in anybody's mind but that the elopers had the necklace. Applebury would think his cousin had come back and got it. If I ever saw anything that looked like plain sailing, I saw it then.

"I got the necklace without any trouble, and went back to the box room to dress in those filthy working clothes you found me in. These I've got on are too damned light colored and conspicuous for a getaway of that sort.

"Then I came back to the head of the stairs and stopped short. Somebody was doing a regular sentry go in the hall below, back and forth, back and forth. I thought he'd get tired of it pretty soon and I'd hear a door shut somewhere and know the coast was clear. But I didn't. I don't know who it was nor what he was doing it for, but he kept it up until daylight. So I had to go back and hide again."

He must have read something in our faces, for he turned once more to Punch.

"Don't tell me *that* was you too!" he snapped.

Punch nodded. "I wasn't waiting for you, though," he said. "I didn't have my rifle or anything."

"Oh, my God!" cried Raglan, with as deep a concentration of bitterness as I've ever heard in human voice.

"Well, I know now," he went on after a while, addressing Mr. Smith, "what my real mistake was. And I swear to God I'll never make it again. I'll never tackle another job where there are any damned boys on the premises."

"You know, that, I believe," said Mr. Smith, "is a perfectly sound idea."

But Raglan was past being wooed back into a good humor.

"I'm sick of this damned country anyhow," he declared. "The profession's being ruined by a lot of young hop-heads, hooligans, stick-up boys who shoot first and try to think afterward and find they haven't brains enough. It's no place for a gentleman, that's the trouble with this country. I'm going abroad again."

"After you've served out your sentence for this affair, I suppose you mean," said Mr. Smith.

"Served out my sentence!" Raglan laughed. "I'll go by the next boat. You're going to take me down-stairs now, aren't you, and see me out through the front door? And if you're wise, you'll send for a car to take me back to town."

"Punch," said Mr. Smith, "go find your Uncle Alexander."

Punch was gone in a flash.

Something else flashed too. Raglan saw it before I did and stiffened in his chair. Old Mr. Smith, with a steady hand, was pointing his automatic pistol straight at his head.

"Don't be a fool," said Raglan.

"I don't intend to be," said Mr. Smith.

"Then listen," said the thief. "Do you think I've been in this house four days without knowing what's been going on in it? I know enough queer things about this family to put it on the blink for the next twenty years. I tell you what I'll do unless you let me go, and let me go damn quick. I'll *confess*. Just ask the women, any one of them, how they'll like that. I know what I'm talking about."

Any notion I may have had that I'd found in Raglan an example of that romantic type endeared to the popular mind by scores of detective stories, a gentleman who has taken to a life of crime, but remains a gentleman none the less, had been dissipated during the past two minutes. The fellow, for all his airs, was nothing but a shabby-minded rascal. He had told us his story partly out of vanity, no doubt, but in the pretty confident hope that we could be blackmailed into letting him go free. I'll confess to the pusillanimous notion that perhaps we'd better.

I couldn't tell what Mr. Smith thought. He said, with a perfectly expressionless face, "You don't know the Corbin family as well as you think you do." But, after all, this committed him to nothing, and he was interrupted before he could go any further.

It was a thump rather than a knock that we heard at the door just then. I guessed who it was, gathered up my crutches, and went and opened it. There sat old Mrs. Corbin in her wheel chair, unattended. She must have run herself up in the elevator.

"You've taxed my curiosity beyond what it would bear," she announced grimly. "I hope what you've got for me, in here, is worth my coming up to look at."

It was an immense relief to me that she had come, and even more that she'd arrived on the scene ahead of her son. It was, after all, for her to decide what was to be done with our disgusting captive.

She turned a long stare upon him, and evidently saw him, despite his fine feathers, for exactly what he was, for, without a word of enlightenment either from Mr. Smith or from me, she said, "So this is the thief Punch has been thinking about for the whole of the past week? I'm glad he's been brought to light."

"Raglan is well up to the top of his class as a gem thief," Mr. Smith now explained. "I've known him and his exploits for years. But since Punch caught him and we took the necklace away from him he seems to have turned his thoughts from burglary to blackmail."

"Blackmail, eh?" the old woman echoed, with a sardonic grin. "Well, you may tell him there's nothing in it. It's never worth while paying money to a blackmailer, since no one with decency enough to stay bought overnight will offer his silence for sale."

"Exactly," Mr. Smith agreed. "Raglan has been hidden," he went on, "most of the time since Wednesday, in the trunk closet on this floor. It appears that this room has certain acoustical peculiarities...."

"Been eavesdropping, has he—on me and Victoria? Well, he's welcome to tell his story to anyone he can get to listen. I don't like to look at him. Can't he be tied up and put out of sight somewhere till he can be taken to jail?"

Alec's arrival just then answered the question. Punch, who came back with him, had told him enough of the story to obviate the need of further explanations.

Raglan was looking venomous by now. He was evidently under a heavy temptation to free his mind. But Alexander Corbin had a way with him which, to one constitutionally averse to violence, must have been overpowering. He didn't take the trouble to tie the rascal; merely ordered him to stick his hands as deep as he could in his trousers pockets and walked him off at the muzzle of his revolver.

"Have some of the men take him to the lock-up in the village," Mrs. Corbin told Alec, "and come back as soon as you've disposed of him. You'll find us in my sitting-room down-stairs."

Punch was for following his uncle and the prisoner, but the old lady called him back.

"I shall want you," she said. Then she asked what time it was.

I wouldn't have believed my watch, had not Mr. Smith's majestic timepiece confirmed the fact that it was only nine o'clock in the morning. Heavens, what a day! It had begun for me when Judy whispered my name through the window just before dawn, a bare five hours ago. Already it seemed a week. And there were people in this house now, plenty of them, just waking up and thinking lazily about breakfast; people to whom it still figured as the wedding day of Judith Corbin and Bruce Applebury!

I must have uttered some sort of consternated exclamation, for old Mrs. Corbin nodded at me with a grim smile. "This is only the beginning of it," she said. "Go down and have breakfast, both of you, and then come up at ten o'clock to my sitting-room. I'm an old woman—worse than old—and I can't put things off. I must settle them now, while I can. Take me down to my room, Punch."

CHAPTER XIX

THE AUTOCRAT

We made a rather silent meal, served imperturbably by Belden. I found myself wondering whether that perfect butler's manner would survive the events which this volcanic day was likely to bring forth. Did he foresee, or even allow himself to guess, what they might be? If I'd been alone with him I would have sounded him out, since he and I are friends of long standing, but in the presence of a comparative stranger like Mr. Smith it wasn't possible.

Just as we finished Victoria came in and the old gentleman, perceiving that she wanted to talk to me, withdrew with his cigar for a stroll in the veranda. She wasted no time after he had gone.

"You don't owe me any favors," she began candidly. "I haven't been any too decent to you, lately, but I believe you'll help all the same."

"I'm glad you believe that," I told her. "I wish you wouldn't think of me as unfriendly. I'll be glad to do all I can to help you as soon as I know what it is that wants to be done."

"There's only one possible thing to do," she asserted urgently. "There can't be two opinions about that; not two sane opinions. And if we're going to save anything at all out of the wreck we've got to do it at once. But it can't be done—nothing can be done—till my mother-in-law can be persuaded to consent to it. You know she won't listen to me—so I'm putting it up to you."

"I still don't know what the thing is," I told her. "If it aims in any way at a reconciliation between Judy and Bruce Applebury, looking toward their marriage...."

She interrupted me with a sharp laugh. "We're long past that," she answered me. "They're leaving, the whole crowd, on the eleven o'clock train to town. Do you wonder?"

"Not a bit. They'll have had enough of the Wild West, that crowd, to last them another ten generations. Think of the myth that will grow up among them, to terrify wayward little Appleburys with."

Victoria smiled at that in spite of herself.

"Oh, if you want to joke about it...." she said petulantly.

"You don't regret it, do you?" I asked. "You love Judy, and you know her. You wouldn't want her to marry a man like that!"

"Oh, I suppose not," she admitted. "He shouldn't have told her, when he did, that he'd lent me money. And of course he shouldn't have tried to make us think that Bill had stolen the necklace.

"But what's the good talking about that? Do you realize what's supposed to happen today? There are more than a thousand people who've been invited to this wedding. There's a special train coming down from town. It's to leave at two o'clock. And there'll be hundreds coming from all around the county in cars.

"There's just one thing to do, unless we mean to have Belden meet them at the gate and send them home. Judy's grandmother's got to be suddenly ill. She could be easily enough. Everybody knows about her. With all this excitement it's likely to happen before night, anyhow.

"But if she'll agree to it now, within the next half-hour or so, we can call up all the afternoon papers in town and tell them the wedding's been postponed on account of it. We can cancel the special train and have someone at the station to tell them about it. We can telephone to a lot of people who'd be driving, and Belden can turn back the rest. The real story will get around, of course, but that won't matter so much. Even the people here in the house will have to pretend to believe what we tell them."

"Have you outlined that plan to Mrs. Corbin?" I asked.

"That's all it would need to make her turn it down," she said hotly. "Even if it had been her own idea, she'd jump to something else—heaven only knows what. I want you to put it up to her."

"Does Judy agree to it?"

I perceived that she evaded this question. "It was Judy's own idea when she wrote me that note, last night," she pointed out. "I don't see how she could object to it now."

I reflected that a good deal of water had gone under the bridge since Judy had written that note. I told Victoria that the plan sounded reasonable to me and that if nothing better turned up at the council the old lady had called, for ten o'clock—it was nearly that now—I'd advocate it.

She was bitterly disappointed at my answer, chose to regard it as a refusal, but it was the best I could do.

"She ought to be given something that would put her to sleep for the day. She's drunk, that's what she is—oh, with excitement, I mean. There's simply no telling what she'll do."

I agreed with the latter part of this statement. I wouldn't put anything beyond the old woman in her present mood, and I didn't blame Victoria for feeling jumpy.

"She's shown herself pretty competent, so far this morning," I pointed out, for whatever consolation there might be in that. "If she can keep it up she may leave our practical wisdom looking foolish."

Victoria showed her opinion of this prophecy by getting up and leaving me.

"Do you know where Judy is now?" I asked.

She paused to say, "No, I don't."

"How about Bill Grant?" I persisted. "Has anything been heard from him?"

"He came back about an hour ago," she said. "Perhaps Belden could find him for you."

I gave up further inquiry at that, mounted my crutches and joined Mr. Smith. It still lacked a minute or two of our appointed hour with Mrs. Corbin.

A car came coasting down the drive and I stared at it with a curiosity that was admissible, I think, since it happened to be my own. I hadn't ordered it, certainly. My interest shot up to excitement when I saw who was getting out of it.

"It's young Mills, the parson from the village," I told Mr. Smith in answer to his inquiring glance. "I gave Bill Grant a card to him this morning. Do you suppose *that's* what our old friend is up to?"

"I never entertained a doubt of it," he said.

The three of us, Mr. Smith, the parson, and I, went up-stairs together to the old lady's sitting-room. Young Mills, though perfectly equal to the situation, was obviously rather tense and his manner was highly professional. We found, already gathered in the room, Bill Grant and Judy, Alec, Victoria and Punch. Mrs. Corbin sat just as I had seen her at our earlier meeting that morning. Miss Digby stood behind her chair.

No one was speaking when we came in, but I guessed from Victoria's flushed cheeks that, despairing of my aid, she'd tried to get a hearing for her own plan and failed.

"These two young people," Mrs. Corbin said, indicating Judy and Bill, "tell me they're fond of each other and want to be married. They've had the grace to ask for my consent, and I've given it. So they're going to be married now. After they're married, if there's anything left to talk about, we can talk."

Victoria's silence at this was as eloquent as the best of Cicero's orations against Catiline, but the old woman remained unmoved by it.

"Is there anyone else, anyone in the house," she asked Judy, "whom you'd like to invite to your wedding?"

"I'd like Belden," the girl answered. And Punch was despatched to fetch him.

We waited in silence until Punch came back with him. The old butler's face was by no means inexpressive, but the emotion most conspicuously absent from it was surprise.

"Now, Mr. Mills," said old Mrs. Corbin.

And so Judy was married to her lover, without the aid of a string orchestra on the lawn or a light opera chorus of bridesmaids—not in any respect as the event had been rehearsed the afternoon before. But Judy seemed completely satisfied with it.

She turned, I was glad to see, from her husband's embrace to her mother, and Victoria, after a moment during which my heart had stood still, gathered the girl up with a sob of surrender into her arms. I don't think there was a word said between them, but words weren't needed. The deplorably long strain was relaxed—temporarily, anyhow.

Judy turned away with her eyes full of tears.

"Where's the guardian angel?" she asked, with a shaky laugh. "I can't see very well."

Bill knew whom she wanted and pushed Punch into her arms.

"You don't mind very much, do you, now?" she demanded. "It makes a difference, doesn't it?"

"Oh, yes," said Punch, wriggling a little under the ordeal of being publicly kissed. "I don't mind as long as it's Bill."

"I don't either," she told him. "It's surprising what a difference it makes."

And then she went the rounds and kissed the rest of us. When she had finished us off she went back to her place. "There!" she said, contentedly.

At that Victoria emerged; got her head, so to speak, above water again.

"It's twenty minutes past ten," she proclaimed, "and we haven't decided anything yet."

Old Mrs. Corbin grinned at that. Apparently she regarded the event of the last few minutes as highly decisive. But she was feeling too good-humored to be captious just then.

"There's the item of the necklace," she remarked. "I suppose that may as well be disposed of now as later. Let's have it, Punch."

Punch, for the last time it's safe to say, took it out of his trousers pocket and handed it to his grandmother.

"I gave this to Judy," she said. "But she and her husband both take the view that I bought it back when I wrote Mr. Bruce Applebury a check, this morning, for twenty-five thousand dollars. Judy says she'd rather have some less exciting sort of wedding present. Well, I'm willing to fall in with her views."

She dangled the glorious thing thoughtfully in her old fingers.

"Punch has been proved right about the old safe," she went on. "That's evidently no place for it, especially as I've been known to forget to lock it up. Anyhow it's been mine for more than half a century, and that's long enough."

With a sudden gesture of resolution she held it out to Victoria.

"Do you want it?" she asked. "Will you take it from me now? Call it a peace offering, if you like."

There was a pretty exciting moment after that. Victoria was so nearly stupefied by the unexpectedness of her mother-in-law's act that she could at first neither speak nor come up to take the thing. My private belief is that it was a knife edge whether the old woman wouldn't snatch it back. She hated giving it up, I'm sure. But she wouldn't have found much satisfaction in keeping it in the bank, and I think, too, she was tired of the long quarrel.

The situation resolved itself at length. Victoria came out of her daze, accepted the thing, and made all the proper acknowledgments. And at the end of them, impulsively and a good deal more simply, she said, "I hope we won't quarrel any more."

"Be reasonable," said the old lady grimly. "Say, half as much."

Victoria laughed and fastened the pearls around her neck. We all crowded around her and admired them in a buzz of talk. It was silenced presently by old Mrs. Corbin's voice.

"If there's nothing more to dispose of," she said, "and I can't see that there is, I think I'll excuse everybody but Miss Digby and take my nap."

"But—" Victoria cried aghast, "we haven't settled *anything* yet. It's half past ten and we haven't even called up the papers, nor cancelled the special train. We don't even know yet what we're going to tell people."

"What should we tell them? Why should we cancel the train? Let them come and see for themselves."

"Do you mean," Victoria demanded aghast, "that we should let everybody we know come down here for the wedding, and then turn them away at the gate with the word that there isn't going to be any?"

"No," said the old woman. "Why turn them away? Bring them in. Feed them, just as we'd meant to do. Introduce them to Mr. and Mrs. William Grant here. Tell them they were married this morning. They'll have to know it some time and it might as well be now."

"But," Victoria cried, voiceless almost with horror, "what will they think?"

"They'll have to think what they please," old Mrs. Corbin declared. "After all, we've lived here a long while and we've always managed our own concerns. We're going to manage this."

<tb>

And that, as of course you know if you remember our newspaper history three months back, is what those Corbins did. There has been, so far as I know, only one event productive of a similar sort of excitement, out in these parts, in living memory.

But this reception at The Oaks was an indisputable victory for the old woman who had willed it. For two hours she sat, very splendidly dressed, in her wheel chair on the lawn like a sovereign on her throne, Belden at her left hand announcing her guests as they came up—superfluously in most instances since her memory for names and faces, especially old names and faces, was astonishingly good. Some she greeted ceremoniously, some with her familiar abruptness, some with an offered hand and some without, but in every case her discrimination was perfect. And in every case, I believe, she passed them on to her son without a word of explanation. She was enjoying it, there can be no doubt of that. Her amazing endurance can't be accounted for otherwise.

Victoria was as good as she was, really superb. I pause to pay tribute to the accuracy of Bill Grant's estimate of her. She would yield, he had predicted, to the proved inevitable. He'll get on with his mother-in-law, that young man.

Well, they got away with it, that's what it all comes to. There wasn't a hint of apology discernible along the line.

The funny thing about it was that it turned out to be so easy. We saw some startled faces, to be sure, and the name Applebury went off, as it were, now and then by mistake. But in the main you wouldn't have known, unless you'd listened to private conversations more closely than one does at a lawn party, that the earth was rocking, or that the stars were about to fall. People chatted, admired the bride, congratulated the groom, ate enthusiastically at the tables grouped around the marquee on the lawn, danced on the canvas that had been stretched over the tennis court—and took their leave.

There was nothing much else, when you come to think of it, that they could have done.

The only unnatural thing about their behavior was the way they departed. Once people had started to go there was a rather panicky sort of rush—like the going-out of the tides of Fundy. It must have been felt that it would be disastrous to be the last one there. By half past six on that lovely June afternoon the lawns were deserted. Well, I don't believe anyone was sorry.

Judy dropped down beside me upon a settee. She'd been looking lovely all the afternoon, I thought, the simplicity of her going-away clothes showing in agreeable contrast to the magnificence of the older women, but now it was over she was white and limp, for the moment an orthodox bride.

"Do you remember when this day began?" she asked. "I'm so tired I can't."

"Don't try," I advised her. "It isn't necessary. It's all—come out in the wash just as you said it would. There's nothing more you even need think about, let alone do."

Victoria, still wearing the necklace, was strolling by with Bill. Punch, very casually, followed along behind.

"I know what she's saying to him," Judy remarked. "She was talking to me about it just now. She wants to know where we're going—on our wedding trip. She seems to think we've got to go somewhere now, tonight—if only to a hotel in town. In order to be—decent, you know."

"I'll tell you where you can go if you don't want to do that," I said. "Go down to my cottage. Just walk off, the two of you, now, any time you like."

"Oh, you darling!" she cried, and put her head down on my shoulder with something like a sob of relief. "Do you mean we can stay there?"

"As long as you like," I told her. "I got things ready, more or less, on the chance, when I went home to lunch. I'll get Mrs. Corbin to take me in up here. You'll find enough to eat to last you till Monday, anyhow."

"Your nice little house," she murmured, "—that I thought I was going to be married in. But this is better."

She sprang up, all trace of fatigue gone.

"Bill," she called.

Victoria followed them into the house.

Punch dropped down beside me.

"Well," he said, "it's been a perfectly wonderful three days, hasn't it? I don't suppose I'll ever have anything as exciting as that happen again. But I'm sort of glad it's over. Only, where do you suppose mother's going to keep the necklace till she can put it in the bank on Monday?"

"I don't know," I said. "But if she tells you I shall never forgive her. You can trust her with it, anyhow. She won't lose it."

"No," said Punch contentedly, "I guess she won't."

THE END

www.ingramcontent.com/pod-product-compliance
Lightning Source LLC
Chambersburg PA
CBHW011448170626
46816CB00008B/2572